EVANGELINE BROWN
and the CADILLAC MOTEL

EVANGELINE BROWN

and the

CADILLAC MOTEL

• •

Michele Ivy DAVIS

DUTTON CHILDREN'S BOOKS · New York

Library of Congress Cataloging-in-Publication Data
Davis, Michele Ivy.
Evangeline Brown and the Cadillac Motel / by Michele Ivy Davis.—1st ed.
p. cm.
Summary: Depicts the unconventional life of an eleven-year-old girl
with her widowed, alcoholic father in a Florida motel.
ISBN 0-525-47221-5
[1. Fathers and daughters—Fiction. 2. Alcoholism—Fiction.
3. Hotels, motels, etc.—Fiction. 4. Florida—Fiction.] I. Title.
PZ7.D2956Ev 2004 [Fic]—dc22 2003021562

Published in the United States by Dutton Children's Books,
a division of Penguin Young Readers Group
345 Hudson Street, New York, New York 10014
www.penguin.com

Designed by Heather Wood

Printed in USA • First Edition

1 3 5 7 9 10 8 6 4 2

For my
MOTHER
and for the
EVANGELINE
BROWNS
of the world

EVANGELINE BROWN
and the CADILLAC MOTEL

CHAPTER 1

I've lived in Paradise all my life.

Paradise. Sounds pretty, don't it? That's the name of this town, though I can't for the life of me imagine why. I figure whoever named it must have been out in the Florida heat too long. Either that, or the *real* Paradise is full of dust and dirt and rotting buildings, too. I hate to think it might be, and I'll be truly disappointed if it really is.

My pa's Cadillac Motel is on Celestial Avenue. It's a long, low coral-colored building—one of those motels where people park in front of their room and the air conditioner sticks out of the wall by the door and drips water on the cement.

There's no missing it. It's right between BAIL BONDS—24 HOURS and all of the bicycles and junk on the sidewalk outside Gus's Pawnshop. Then there's this big metal arrow sign full of lightbulbs pointing right to the office. The arrow is supposed to flash at night, but most of the bulbs are burned out. AIR CONDITIONED. TV. VACANCY. Those words still work.

But the real reason you can't miss the Cadillac Motel is the big butt end of the pink Cadillac. It looks like it's crashed partway through the cinder-block wall of the motel office. Only the trunk and tail fins stick out, and the lights in back go on and off. That was Pa's idea. He said it would get more customers, but I sure wish he hadn't thought of it. I had enough to deal with, what with living in a motel and all, and the kids at school, well, they just wouldn't leave me alone about that pink Cadillac butt. So I don't mess with them anymore, and they don't mess with me. I do just fine on my own.

In the summer I mostly read my library books, but lots of times I help Ruby clean the motel rooms, especially when she brings me some of her chocolate cookies. That woman sure can cook! Course, anyone could tell that just by looking at her. She's got little sausage fingers and sausage arms and little sausage legs that end in teeny-tiny feet. I don't know how they keep her up. Her husband, Wendell, looks just the same.

Ruby cleaned rooms for Pa from the beginning, when him and Mama bought the Cadillac Motel. I was a baby then. After Mama died, it was just Ruby and Pa and me. Ruby would bring us leftovers to heat for supper the next day and wash Pa's and my clothes in the Laundromat across the street when she washed the sheets from the motel. Sometimes she'd get us groceries when Pa gave her money for them; otherwise, I just ran over to the little store a couple of blocks away. The stuff in that place was so dusty, I figure it must be at least a hundred years old, but we haven't died from it yet.

Me and Ruby get along pretty good because she's not a hugger. That sits just fine with me. I don't like to be hugged, and sometimes fat old ladies just want to squeeze the bejeezers out of you.

"Time you started thinking about school," Ruby said one August morning as we ripped the sheets off a bed. "Summer's almost over."

She didn't need to remind me, but her words felt like a fist punching me in my gut. I picked the sheets up off the brown rug and jammed them hard into a dirty pillowcase.

I hated school. It was so boring I could hardly stand it. Maybe it was because of my library books, but I already knew most of the stuff, and if I didn't, I learned it real quick—quicker than the other kids, I guess, because the teachers would repeat things until I'd like to shrivel up and die.

And this year was going to be the worst. Probably the rottenest year in history, because Mrs. Thornton was going to be my teacher. I already knew her from when she was in charge of the playground. I'd be minding my own business when all of a sudden she'd holler "Eddie Brown!" Then she'd stomp on over to me in those black, laced-up man shoes of hers, marching so hard across the playground that the glasses on the string around her neck would jump. She told me I was a troublemaker and that we had a personality conflict. I wasn't sure what that meant, but if it meant we hated each other's guts, well, I guess it was probably true.

I wanted to move away before school started because there was no getting away from her this time. There was only one sixth-grade class, and she was the only sixth-grade teacher. I even asked Pa if we could move, but he said no, the motel was our home. Well, he didn't have to be in a class with nasty Mrs. Thornton all day, or he'd have moved in a minute.

"You hear me?" Ruby asked as she pulled the spread over the bed. "Only a couple more weeks till school starts. Better let your pa know you need some clothes." She smoothed the bedspread over the pillows while I threw the sheets into the hamper. "I'll take you to Tina's on Thursday after I finish here." She sat on the edge of the bed and fanned herself. "Doesn't look to me like anything you own still fits. Tell him you need shoes, too."

I looked down at my scruffy tennis shoes and knew she was right. No sense in giving those kids at school anything else to tease me about.

When we finished up, I took my library book off the laundry cart and went to look for Pa. He was sitting on one of the rusty green chairs in the shade outside the motel office, drinking a beer like he usually did in the afternoon. There were a couple of empty cans beside him.

"Pa?" I said when I got close.

He squinted up at me and gave me a little grunt.

"Ruby says I need some clothes for school, and she'll

take me." I hated to ask for money with things being so tight and all.

I think he was ready to tell me there wasn't any money to give, but I guess the way my ankles stuck out of my jeans and the bones on my wrists poked out of my sleeves made him change his mind. He got up and went inside to get some money out of the cash box behind the counter. When he came back out, he handed me a few bills.

"Now don't spend too much," he said, sitting back down and picking up his beer.

"Yes, Pa. And thank you." I knew to be polite to Pa when he handed out money because it didn't happen that often. I carefully put the money between the pages of my book so I'd have it ready come Thursday.

Pa leaned forward in his chair, trying to look down the street. "You see Jesse coming?" he asked.

Jesse fixed cars in the old garage at the corner and was a friend of Pa's. They knew each other while they were growing up in another town. His kid, Farrell, had moved to Paradise with him about a month before and was supposed to be about my age, but even though Pa and Jesse hung out together at the motel or the garage and drank their beer and whiskey, Jesse's kid never came around. Not ever.

"How come I never see your boy?" I asked Jesse once.

Jesse just yawned and said, "Farrell's not one for being with people much. He likes to keep to himself."

I guess that was true, because I surely never saw him. I wondered how come and thought maybe there was something wrong with him, or maybe he wasn't quite right in the head.

But that didn't stop Pa and Jesse from being together all the time, or Pa from waiting for Jesse outside the motel most afternoons like he was now. I looked down the street.

"No, Pa," I said. "Can't see Jesse coming."

I was ready to go inside when I caught sight of a boy I'd never seen before out in front of the garage.

CHAPTER 2

I wondered if the boy I saw was Jesse's kid. He looked about my age and was bouncing a basketball. I thought about what Jesse had said about him. If this Farrell kid was a strange one, I needed to be careful. I didn't want to get too close, but I did want to check him out and especially get a good look at that basketball he had. Maybe it belonged to him.

First I hid around the edge of the building behind the oil barrels and rusty car parts Jesse left lying around, trying not to trip over them and make a noise—I didn't want the boy to hear me coming.

He stood in the entrance of the garage between a couple of cars and began throwing the basketball against the cinder-block wall. Sometimes he'd aim it at the bars on the windows like he was trying to break them, but mostly he aimed at loose pieces of peeling blue paint and knocked them off. He was pretty good at it.

I watched him till I got bored. He didn't look all that strange to me, so I marched right up to him.

"You Farrell?" I asked.

"Yep." He didn't look at me, just kept on bouncing the ball against the wall.

"That all you got to say?"

"Yep," he said. Bam, bam, bam went the ball, echoing against the wall. He never looked anywhere but at that stupid ball.

I stood there for a couple of minutes and tried again. "You play basketball?"

"Nope." Then he stopped bouncing the ball and looked at me. He hardly blinked. "What's it to you?"

"Just making conversation," I answered. All of a sudden, I decided this whole checking-out-the-strange-kid thing wasn't such a good idea, and I'd better hustle back to the motel.

"*You* play basketball?" he asked. I stopped.

"Sure," I said, eyeing the ball. "In school." All of a sudden I wanted to grab that basketball of his. It seemed I was born wishing for my own basketball. I'd asked Pa for one lots of times, and he'd always say "Sure," but he never got me one. I guess he didn't have the money, or else he kept forgetting.

"How come you got a basketball and you don't play?" I asked, thinking about the unfairness of it all.

"I said I *don't* play. I *did*, at my old school." He sounded like he was explaining something to a little kid. That really got my goat. I was ready to tell him off when he held the ball out to me.

"Want to toss a few?"

Boy, that cooled my anger in a hurry. I took the ball and bounced it a few times. It was a good one, with just the right amount of air. I aimed for an imaginary basket over the open garage door and let it fly. It went through the hoop without touching—or it would have if there'd been a hoop. Farrell caught it and tossed it back to me. I aimed again. Perfect shot. Third time's a charm, I said to myself as I threw it—the beginning of a perfect arc. But just as I was going to make a winning basket, a breeze came up and pushed it crooked. It sailed through the open garage door and bounced across the filthy floor to where Jesse was.

Jesse was shimmying out from under an old Chevy when the ball landed right next to him, in the pan he'd just used to change the oil. Black oil splashed up on him and his greasy coveralls, and all over the car he was working on. He scrambled the rest of the way out, rubbing his face and smearing the dirty stuff all over it.

"Get the hell out of here!" he shouted, coming at us and roaring so loud it hurt my ears. "Get the hell out of here, and don't come back!" He threw that oily basketball at us with all his might. It made black splotches on the driveway where it bounced.

Jesse was really big, and he scared me half to death when he was mad. I turned and ran as fast as I could. Farrell ran, too, catching the ball mid-bounce without even slowing down. He was right behind me when I got to the motel, and we didn't slow down until we'd run around the end of the building and into the backyard.

When we stopped, Farrell dropped the oily ball into a

clump of grass there. He pushed his hair back and rubbed his eyes with the back of his hand. When he turned to look at me, I started to laugh. He had a streak of black across his forehead and black smudges around his eyes. He looked just like a raccoon. I knew I shouldn't laugh at somebody who might not be right in the head. I wasn't at all sure what he was going to do, and I tried to stop, I truly did.

"What are you laughing at, girl?" Farrell demanded. His face was turning red with anger. If he'd been a cartoon, I'll bet his eyes would have bugged out and smoke would have steamed from his ears; he was that mad.

I pointed to his reflection in the window. He turned and stared at it but didn't crack a smile. Slowly he reached down, picked up the end of his shirt, and wiped his eyes.

I'd lived with Pa long enough to know how to keep the peace. "It's all gone now," I said. "I wasn't laughing at you, anyway. I was laughing at your pa. Did you see him? Oil splattered all over him? And smeared all over his face? I think I got him good."

Farrell smiled, the first smile I'd seen on him. Then he laughed a little, but it sounded funny, like it wasn't something he did very often. "Maybe ugly Mrs. Clark will bring in her Mercedes with those white leather seats. . . . Hey. What's your name?"

"Eddie Brown." I was going to leave it at that.

"Eddie? That's a boy's name."

I could feel my temper heating up. "Ed," I said. "For my initials. *E.D.*"

He looked interested. "What do they stand for?"

I gave up. This guy wasn't going to let go. "They stand for Evangeline Dawn. That's my real name, but you'd better call me Eddie," I threatened.

"Evangeline's a real pretty name. Your daddy name you that?"

"My mama did," I said softly.

"Where is she?"

"She died. When I was five."

"Do you remember her?"

"Some. I remember she had a pretty smile and a real restful voice. Sometimes she'd read me stories." I stopped. I was telling too much to somebody I didn't even know. "What about *your* mama?" I asked. "Where's she?"

"She died," Farrell said abruptly. "A long time ago." Then he picked up his basketball and started to leave.

I must have said something wrong, but I couldn't for the life of me think of what it was. All I did was ask about his mama, and he took his basketball and walked away. I needed to do something fast.

"I know where a real basketball hoop is," I called to his back. He stopped but didn't turn. "I'll take you there tomorrow if you want."

"See you around" was all he said. Now what kind of an answer was that?

CHAPTER 3

The next morning I decided to help Ruby for a while since Farrell hadn't shown up anywhere. I found her in the supply room. She had the cart pushed out into the hall and was putting stacks of fresh, white sheets and towels on it.

"I'm almost ready to get started," she said. "Will you fill the soap bucket for me?"

"Sure," I said, picking up the green plastic bucket. I squeezed past her into the supply room and opened a big cardboard box in the corner that was full of those cute little bars of soap. I filled that bucket to the top, even though I knew we wouldn't really need that many. I liked their clean perfume smell.

"What kind of a day is it today?" Ruby asked as I inspected the cans of air freshener. We had lots of different flavors like Country Lilac, Spring Showers, and Floral Morning. I liked the way the names sounded. They made pictures in my mind of places I'd never been, far away from the broiling heat of Florida in the summer.

"It's a Mountain Meadow day for sure," I said, thinking of a clear, cool mountaintop with snow on it and flowers blooming all around—not at all like the flatness of Paradise.

"You ever been to the mountains, Ruby?" I asked as I put the blue can on the cart.

"Nope," she said, shaking her head. "I went to Niagara Falls once but never did get to the mountains." She closed the supply room door with a bang.

"OK. Let's get to work," she said, pushing the heavy cart to the first room. I followed with the vacuum. Ruby knocked on the door a few times real hard and yelled, "Housekeeping!" even though she knew the room was empty. "Never can be too careful," she said as she unlocked the door with her ring of keys and went inside.

I didn't mind helping Ruby during the summer. It gave me something to do to fill my vacation time besides reading my books. Anyway, cleaning the rooms didn't take nearly as long as it used to. A few years ago we'd get lots of customers, regulars who did the craft shows or flea markets, or truckers who just wanted a shower and a place to sleep. But the Highway Department built a bypass. Pa kind of let the place fall apart, so now the paint was peeling at the bottom of the walls where the rain splashed in summer, and green stuff was growing under the air conditioners. I guess the customers are staying someplace else now.

Before I followed Ruby in, I looked down the row of rooms to the office that stuck out at the end of the motel. I could see Pa behind the counter. I liked mornings because he was up and working, just like everybody else's pa. Later on in the day he'd start taking beer breaks with Jesse, and by suppertime, he'd be passed out on the couch, and there was no talking to him. That probably had something to do with why the regular customers didn't come back, too.

Me and Ruby zipped through the rooms that morning, opening the curtains to let the daylight in, changing the sheets, and spraying the air freshener everywhere. Even though it was my own pa's motel, I had to admit that those rooms did stink. They smelled like a mix of old cigarette smoke and mildew, and nothing much we did could get that smell out. Maybe it was stuck in the carpet and heavy curtains, maybe even in the paneling each room had on the wall above the head of the bed. So every day I sprayed the freshener and hoped the room would smell like clean mountain air or wildflowers when a customer came. But it never did.

After me and Ruby took the sheets to the Laundromat, I heard the sound of Farrell's basketball coming from down the street at the garage. I strolled on over, not wanting to look too interested in that ball.

"How're you doing, Farrell?" I asked between slaps as he dribbled it down the driveway.

He ignored me, turned, and tossed the ball against the garage wall.

"I said, 'HOW'RE YA DOING, FARRELL?'" Even

though traffic was going by making noise and blowing up dust, I knew he heard me, and that aggravated me no end. He bounced the ball a few more times, then stopped right in front of me.

"Where is this hoop you were bragging on yesterday?" he asked.

"I don't brag," I told him, "but I'll take you there if you'll let me play, too."

He considered me for a minute and then nodded. I guess he was thinking a hoop with a girl was better than no hoop at all. "Let's go," he said.

Now, I could have taken him the long way, twisting and turning around the neighborhood so he couldn't find it by himself, but in a few weeks school would start, and he'd be wise to me anyway. Besides, he had the ball, and I surely wanted to try a few real hoops while none of the kids from school were around and Mrs. Thornton wasn't on the playground.

"Where's this go?" he asked as I led him down an overgrown concrete path with rusty chain-link fence on both sides. I didn't slow down or turn around; I just grunted and led on. This time *I* was in charge. Let *him* see what it felt like when somebody didn't answer.

When we came to the gate at the school yard, it had a padlock on it. I climbed over easy. I didn't hear Farrell coming over after me, so I stopped and turned around.

"Come on," I called.

He just stood there. I sighed and went back to the fence.

"What's your problem?" I asked. "Come on over."

He was looking at the fence and jiggling the ball real nervous-like in his hands. His face was pale, and he kept licking his lips.

"Come *on,*" I said. "The hoop is just over there." I pointed to the basketball part of the school yard. The hoop was out of sight in the shade of a tree, one of those big ones with Spanish moss dripping from the branches.

Farrell took a deep breath, grabbed hold of the fence, closed his eyes, and hustled over.

"What's with you?" I asked when he stood beside me. "You afraid of fences or something?"

Farrell looked at me for a second and then dashed away, bouncing that basketball like there was no tomorrow. I ran after him, and pretty soon we were sinking baskets right and left. We were a match, and I kept up with him, even though he was taller than me. After a while he forgot to be serious, and we were laughing and shouting and having a good old time. When the heat finally got to us, we headed for the shade and flopped down on a little patch of grass under the tree.

"Why do they lock the playground?" he asked.

"Keeps kids out," I answered.

"That's stupid. It's a school playground, for Christsake."

"Don't swear," I told him sharply. Pa washed my mouth out with one of those little bars of soap anytime I learned a new swearword. It tasted disgusting.

"Well, why do they lock it up?"

"School's out, that's why. Gangs, drugs, and other stuff

happens here, especially at night. Of course, it don't keep 'em out, but it makes it harder. See those backyards over there? When the people that live there complain and the police come, they can catch the troublemakers easy. Like shooting fish in a barrel, Pa says."

Farrell grunted and lay on his back. I leaned back, too, and studied the leaves in the tree.

"You afraid of fences?" I asked again. I was feeling a little drowsy from the heat and all our running.

"Not fences," he answered quietly.

I turned my head a little and saw his eyes were closed.

"Then what?" I asked.

"Being closed in."

"You mean like with a fence around you?"

"Yep."

"Why?"

He didn't answer for a long time, and I turned my head full on to look at him. His brown hair was plastered to his forehead with sweat, and his cheeks were red from the heat. I watched his faded T-shirt go up and down as he breathed; I thought he'd fallen asleep.

"Because of one of the places they sent me when my ma died," he finally said, his voice startling me in the quiet.

I turned on my side. How could going someplace make him scared of being closed in? "Where'd they send you?"

He opened his eyes and turned his head toward me, then looked away. "Never mind," he said. "I don't want to talk about it."

"Why not?"

I waited, but he didn't say anything else. He just looked up at the tree. That really annoyed me, because he had sounded just like Pa.

I don't want to talk about it. That's just what Pa would say when I was little and I asked him about my mama. "Pa?" I'd say, looking up at him. "What was Mama like?" Or "Tell me a story about Mama and me when I was a baby."

But he'd frown and say, "I've got things to do," and then he'd walk away. After a while, I just quit asking.

Farrell lay there in the shade and didn't say anything else. I sighed and turned over onto my back. Nobody ever wanted to talk about anything important.

CHAPTER 4

On Thursday, school shopping day, Ruby finished up her chores early.

"Go wash your face and comb your hair," she said as she came back from the Laundromat and carried the clean sheets to the storage room. "And be sure your socks don't have holes in them."

I rushed to my room and pulled off my shoes. The right sock had a hole in it, so I had to get all of my socks out of the drawer to find a good one. I took a washcloth to my face and a comb to my hair and hurried out to the office. Ruby was sitting on one of the orange plastic chairs along the wall, drinking a soda.

It took her a few minutes, but she finally managed to get herself standing.

"You look real nice," she said. I handed her the money,

and we walked down the street to Tina's Thrift Shop. Even though she kind of waddled and was always fanning herself, I pretended that we were just another mother and daughter out shopping for school clothes.

Tina, the lady who owned the shop, looked like she belonged in some Hollywood movie. She had this flashy orangish-red hair that looked like they'd mixed a bad batch of dye in the drugstore. Only thing was, it'd been the same color for as long as I could remember. Tina's lipstick usually matched her hair. But what truly amazed me was that she wore these huge, dangling earrings. It's a wonder they didn't catch on something and rip her ears off, or that the holes where she stuck them weren't big enough to put pennies through. I checked every time, but they always just looked normal.

Tina's shop had this musty smell that always hit me when I walked in—I guess from all the clothes. It could make my eyes water. But not counting that, it really wasn't bad for a thrift store. In the front window were glass shelves where she kept fancy glasses and vases. Sometimes the sun would shine in, and all of the glass things would light up—red, green, blue. It was like a rainbow in that window.

Kids' clothes hung on special racks, and Tina's had two little dressing rooms with flowered curtains where people could try things on. I hated trying things on, though, because I didn't like to stand behind the curtain in my underwear. What if somebody came into my little dressing room by mistake or the wind blew the curtain open? And I didn't like my feet and legs showing below the curtain either. I really wished Tina had doors on her dressing rooms, but I guess sometimes you've got to suffer to get new clothes.

I'm partial to blue jeans and T-shirts myself, but Ruby was always trying to put me in frilly, lacy things. You'd think she'd have learned by now, but she hadn't. When I peeked out the side of the curtain, there was Ruby holding a purple blouse with a ruffle around the neck and flowers down the front. I could have puked.

"I don't want it, Ruby," I said from behind the curtain as I pulled on my jeans. "You hear me?"

She didn't say anything. I could hear her stand there for a minute, then sigh and march away.

I was real happy as Tina stuffed my new jeans and T-shirts in the bag. It wasn't until that night when I unpacked it that I saw the ruffled blouse at the bottom. Well, I'll tell you, Ruby could grow old and die before I'd ever wear that thing.

After Tina's Thrift Shop, me and Ruby went to Woolworth's and got me some new tennis shoes and socks. The shoes were so white they hurt my eyes, and the big bunch of socks would last me a good while. They were all the same, so if one got a hole in it, I could just pull out another one.

We got some notebooks and pens and a big stack of fresh, lined paper. That's the only part of school I *do* like—starting out with all that blank paper and notebooks. Seems like anything can happen then. It's almost like starting over again each fall. Of course, after about a week the new is all gone, and everything is the same as it always was; but for a few days, anything is possible.

"You ready for school?" I asked Farrell the next time I saw him. "You going to the same one I go to?"

"Yep," he said. "I'll probably be in your grade. I got held back once." He didn't sound happy. I guess he was nervous about starting school in a new place and not knowing anybody. I'd been at that school my whole life, and at least I knew which kids to steer clear of. I decided not to tell him about Mrs. Thornton.

"I got new books and paper," I said.

"Not me. My old stuff is still good."

"Well, did you get paper?"

"Don't need any," he said.

"I'll share with you," I offered. "I've got lots."

He studied the rock he was kicking with his toe. "Thanks," he said, but he didn't smile.

I could see this wasn't going to be an easy year for either of us.

CHAPTER 5

On the first day of school, I passed Farrell sitting in the principal's office. He was slouched down in a hard wooden chair, his legs stretched out in front of him and an old blue notebook on his lap. He didn't see me because he was looking around the room like he was memorizing where the doors and windows were so he could make a quick getaway. I guess he was waiting for Mr. Miller to check him in and tell him which class to go to. I wondered why he had on the same jeans he wore when we played with his basketball. They were kind of grubby, and the threads were hanging off them at the bottom.

I walked down the hall that was all shiny from a good summer polishing, and through the open door of the sixth-grade classroom. I went straight to the desk all the way in the back corner by the supply closet. I always sat there. The way

I figured it, the teacher's pets and the smart kids were the ones who sat in the front. Teachers never called on the kids in the back, and that suited me just fine. In my own back corner I could listen if I had a mind to, or draw pictures, or look out the window.

I spent some time making sure I had a good desk and chair—ones that didn't wobble. Mrs. Thornton hadn't come in yet, and I was glad. She could sure spoil a room. She was so old, I figured she'd been at the school since it was built. She never wore makeup and usually went around with her lips clamped tight together in an ugly frown.

I sat down at my desk and started putting my notebook and paper away. The other kids were making lots of noise, but nobody said anything to me. They never did. Then all of a sudden everyone stopped talking and moving around, and the room got quiet. I looked up, and one of the prettiest ladies I'd ever seen walked in. Her dress was soft and silky, and it kind of flowed behind her as she went to the teacher's desk. Her hair had curls in it, and she had on bracelets that jingled when she moved her arm. She wasn't anybody I'd ever seen in town, and I guess nobody else had ever laid eyes on her either because the whole class just stared at her. Joey Johnson poked Fred O'Brien, and they both smiled real big. Nope, she sure wasn't Mrs. Thornton.

"Good morning," the lady said as she leaned against the teacher's desk.

Everyone stared. Nobody moved.

The teacher gave us a funny look and then smiled the

nicest smile at all of us. "I'm Miss Rose, and I'll be your teacher this year."

The kids started chattering at once. Then she held up her hand, and everyone got real quiet. It was like she had a magic wand.

"Mrs. Thornton retired over the summer and moved north, so I've come to teach her class. I know we'll have a lot of fun learning this year."

The whole class nodded with big, silly grins. I guess I wasn't the only one who had a personality conflict with Mrs. Thornton, the old bat.

Just then the classroom door opened, and the principal came in with Farrell, who didn't look happy at all.

"Miss Rose," Mr. Miller said, "this is a new student for your class. His name is Farrell Garrett, and he just moved to town."

I heard the kids around me whisper.

"Looks big and dumb."

"Where'd he get those clothes?"

"Bet they came from a junk pile."

He was the first new kid in the class since I could remember. I never thought about it before, but it seemed like nobody ever came to Paradise. They only left.

I knew Farrell heard the kids whisper about him, but he just frowned, real ferocious, and stared at the floor. I hated them all.

"Children," warned Miss Rose. "Please be quiet." And they were. That was truly an amazing power she had. I'd never seen anything like it. It was like she was some kind of witch. I wondered if she was a good witch, like Glinda, the Good Witch of the North in *The Wizard of Oz*, or if she was really the Wicked Witch of the West in disguise.

"Farrell, you may sit here for a little while," she said, pointing to a desk in the front row. "We're going to rearrange the classroom in a few minutes, and everyone will be changing seats."

Farrell walked to the desk and slumped down in the seat. He never looked around, so I guess he didn't see me sitting at the far end of the room.

When the principal left, Miss Rose walked slowly across the front of the classroom and down along the side by the windows, studying each kid as she passed. I looked down when she came close, hoping she wouldn't notice me. She walked right past and back up the other side by the door.

"First we need to call the roll," she said as she took a spiral teacher's notebook out of her desk drawer and reached back inside for a pen. Nobody had taken roll in years. We'd all been in the school since kindergarten, and the teachers knew who we were.

"Janet Abrams?"

"Here?" Janet said softly, her voice going up at the end so it was like a question. She raised her hand a little and smoothed her hair.

"Selma Adams?"

Selma's hand shot up in the air and she answered, "Here!" loud and clear. I heard some giggling, but a look from Miss

Rose silenced it quick. Everybody was behaving like I'd never seen them. Ours was the worst class ever, according to our other teachers. I guess that proved Miss Rose really did have magic powers.

Next to each name, Miss Rose wrote something in her book. When she called "Evangeline Brown," the whole class turned to look at me.

"I go by Eddie," I said, daring them to make something of it.

"I'll remember that, Eddie," she said, her pencil scratching in her book.

As soon as I said it, I noticed out of the corner of my eye that Farrell straightened up. He didn't turn around, but I could tell he knew I was there.

"Now we're going to do something different," Miss Rose said, putting the teacher's book on her desk. "We'll start the year with everyone sitting in alphabetical order, beginning with the seat next to the door where Farrell is and going across the front of the classroom. Everyone take your belongings and go stand along one of the walls. When I call your name, please come to the desk I am pointing to."

The room was noisy with talking and laughing and chairs sliding away from the desks. Finally everybody was against one wall or another. I just stood up and backed into the corner by my desk. Maybe she wouldn't notice me, and I could stay in my usual seat. I spit on my fingers and crossed them behind my back for luck.

"Eddie Brown? Right here, please." She was pointing to a

desk right smack in the front of the class. How could she even consider it? I liked being by the supply closet. It was my spot, each year, in every grade, in every classroom.

"Eddie?"

I squeezed my notebook and marched to the front row. The lights were brighter there, and I was in plain view of everybody. I felt naked.

Miss Rose, I decided, was definitely a wicked witch in disguise. Mrs. Thornton would have left things the way they were.

"Farrell? Please sit here," Miss Rose said a few minutes later. I looked up to see Farrell sliding into the desk directly behind me. I turned a little, but he didn't pay any attention. I don't think he liked being so close to the front any more than I did.

When everybody was sitting at their new desks, Miss Rose smiled again. Then she said something that hit me like a bomb.

"Since I am new in town," she said, "I'm going to visit each of your homes this fall so I can get to know you better. I want this to be a successful year for us all."

My heart thudded in my ears.

No! I wanted to shout at her. *No, you can't come to my house! I don't want you there! Nobody from school comes to where I live.*

I thought of Pa and the motel and the car butt sticking out of the wall. I remembered second grade when Carol Anne Williams and Janet Abrams came home from school with me. The nasty things they said about me afterward echoed in my head. And now Miss Rose was going to do it. She was going to see it all.

Black dots twinkled in front of my eyes and I was sure I was going to faint. Only the thought of all those kids standing around my body, staring down at me lying on that shiny brown floor, kept me up.

At least she said she was going to start her visits beginning with kids at the end of the alphabet and work her way to the front of it. That would give me some time. But time for what? I didn't know.

CHAPTER 6

Nothing was going the way it should anymore, and there wasn't anything I could do about it. I felt like kicking something. When I got home from school, I took a bag of potato chips from the display stand on the motel counter and a soda from the cooler, even though I wasn't supposed to. Pa said they were for the customers. Well, forget it. There weren't that many customers, and they never bought anything anyway. The stuff was so old it probably had fur growing on it. Besides, if I got sick and died, I wouldn't have to sit in the front of that class ever again.

Farrell walked by the motel bouncing his basketball. He looked like he was headed to the school yard to shoot a few and was in a foul mood, too. I grabbed an extra soda and went after him. Maybe a couple of hours of smashing that basketball would do both of us some good.

It was stifling hot outside—too hot to run to catch up with him. He was too far ahead to yell, and I didn't feel like it anyway. I just walked on my own, the sodas feeling cold and wet in my hands. In the school yard I put them under a tree, with the bag of chips on top to keep it away from the ants. Then, without a word, I ran at Farrell, who was dribbling toward the basket. He hadn't seen me coming, and I grabbed that ball away from him mid-bounce, just as nice as you please. I didn't care. I was still mad at Miss Rose and her classroom changes and her visit plans.

Foolhardy. That's what Ruby would've called me. She'd have been right, too, because Farrell let out a roar and rushed at me. I truly wished I hadn't taken his ball, but I was in it now. I wasn't about to let him know I was scared, though, so I scooted that ball over to the basket just as fast as can be and sunk a beauty—it didn't even touch the rim.

Then Farrell tackled me from behind and pushed me face-first into the dirt.

I had dust in my eyes and a mouth full of sand, and I couldn't breathe. My chest went in and out, and I tried to swallow, but nothing happened. No air came in. Nothing. I turned over and pushed Farrell away from sitting on my chest. I started hitting him with my fists. Finally, he looked down at my face and jumped off. He pulled me up and slapped me across the back a couple of times. I gasped and sputtered, and wonderful, wonderful air filled my lungs.

"What the hell do you think you are doing?" I yelled, never mind the no-swearing rule. "You could've killed me!"

As soon as I said that, his face turned angry, like a churning thundercloud. I didn't care. He *could* have killed me. I slugged him in the stomach as hard as I could. He grabbed me by the hair and pushed me into the dirt again. I kicked any part of him I could reach. He leaned over and held my hands above my head, and I just kept kicking. I got a few good ones in, too. But I was too sweaty and tired and dirty to keep it up. Finally I lay still.

"You through?" Farrell asked, still holding my wrists in a death grip.

I nodded.

"Will you behave if I let you go?"

"Sure," I said. I was already regretting what I had done, and my nose itched something ferocious.

"OK." He loosened his hands.

I slid my wrists out of his grip and sat up, rubbing them.

He sat next to me and pulled them toward him, studying the redness he had put there. "Do they hurt?"

"Not much," I fibbed, pulling them away. "I'm sorry I took your ball."

Farrell got ready to say something, but his lips closed into a tight, straight line instead, and he looked away.

"Me, too," he finally said. He stood up and reached out his hand to pull me up.

"You don't fight too bad for a girl," he said, "but you could use some teaching. You can't just toss your arms and feet out like that and hope to hit something."

I started to tell him I'd managed just fine on my own so far, but he kept on talking.

"If you want, I can show you a few moves sometime. I learned some good ones where I used to live. But first you have to promise you won't try to pick a fight with me again. I could hurt you if I put my mind to it."

I knew he was right, even though I hated to think it. I'd done pretty well up to now, but I hadn't really been in that many fights.

"OK," I answered, dusting off my legs and shirt and wiping sweaty sand from my face. My teeth could feel the grit, and I spit a few times for good measure.

"I have sodas under the tree," I offered, and Farrell gave me a slow smile as he trotted after me. We sat in the shade drinking and sharing the bag of chips.

Miss Rose had sure set us off. She'd only been in school one day, but I could see she was going to be a real trouble-maker.

CHAPTER 7

When I got home from the playground, Pa and Jesse weren't sitting outside the motel drinking beer like they usually did in the afternoon. The green chairs were empty. I peeked through the window of the lobby and saw Pa talking to some lady. She had fancy makeup around her eyes, and her lips were shiny red. Her blond hair was twisted on top of her head, but it looked messy to me because little bits had come loose and were curling next to her face. And she had the longest eyelashes I'd ever seen. I wondered if they were real. I saw some fake ones once in a box in Riley's Drugstore that looked like little caterpillars. Hers looked OK, so it was hard to tell. She wore a tight silvery blouse, a very short skirt, and the skinniest, tallest, reddest high heels I'd ever seen. It's a wonder she could stand on them without falling over. I could just imagine what Ruby would've said about the way she was dressed.

On the linoleum floor on each side of her sat big suitcases. They were made out of pretend leather stuff and had new-looking stickers pasted all over them from faraway places like London and Cairo and Madrid, like she'd just got back from a trip around the world. She didn't fool me, though. I don't think she could have taken the bus to Tallahassee dressed like that, much less gone across the ocean.

The lady and Pa stopped talking when I came through the door.

"Hi, Pa," I said.

Pa nodded to me, but the lady never looked over. Instead, she studied the countertop like there was something really interesting pasted on it. I *knew* what was on it, and it wasn't the least bit interesting—just some oily stains, a worn spot in the front where people leaned when they checked in, and a chip in the tan Formica at the front corner where something had banged into it a long time ago. The lady saw the chip and touched it with her red fingernails. She still didn't look up.

I figured I had interrupted something, so I waited to find out what was going on. They didn't start talking again, though. They both just stood still, like they were frozen in a movie and the film got stuck. I decided I'd wait them out.

Pa finally frowned at me. "Go on inside, Evangeline. There's ice cream in the freezer."

Well, I'll tell you *that* got my attention. We never had ice cream except when Ruby brought it, and even then, we saved it for supper. So if they wanted me to leave, I guess I'd do it for a dish of ice cream.

I went around the counter past Pa and through the open door into our little apartment that was behind the office. Pa always kept the door between the two open so he could hear if anybody came to the motel to register, even if he was watching TV.

The main part of our apartment was really one big room. It had a kitchen at one end and a green couch and chair in front of the TV at the other end. Pa's bedroom door went off the kitchen end of the room, and mine went off the living room end; the bathroom was in between. Three rooms and a bathroom. That's where we lived.

I got a bowl down from the cupboard and filled it full to the top with ice cream. Pa looked like he was going to be out there a while, and I wasn't one to miss the opportunity for a little extra.

I guess Pa and the lady heard the bowl clattering and me moving around because they started talking again in low voices. Now, I figured out a long time ago that when people wait for kids to leave and then talk low so the kids can't hear, they're saying things that are a lot more interesting than any other time.

So I sat at the table for a minute, made a little noise, and rattled some school papers like I was settling down to eat. They talked in whispers for a couple more minutes. Then I guess they figured I was occupied and not paying attention because their voices got more normal. I took off my shoes, silent as can be, so I just had my socks on. Then I picked up my bowl of ice cream and went to sit on the floor with my back to the wall near the open door to the office.

". . . and so I couldn't take it anymore," the lady was saying. "Everything I own is in these two suitcases. He has all my money. I'm never going back. He can rot in hell."

"Now, Mary Ann," Pa said, kind of gentle, which surprised me because I didn't hear him talk like that much anymore. "The rooms here are only rooms. There's no place to cook or anything. They are for staying in, not for living in."

"I could get a hot plate, and I saw a little fridge at Gus's Pawnshop a few days ago. That's all I would need. . . ." Her voice just fizzled out.

I sat there out of sight quietly eating my ice cream, but all the time they were talking, there was this clicking noise coming from the counter.

"I'd park my car out in front of my room," she said. "It's not much to look at, but people will think the motel has regular customers, and that would be good for business."

Click.

"Remember that Alfred Hitchcock movie where the woman gets stabbed in the shower? Ever since that came out, nobody wants to stay in an empty motel. If you let me move in, I'll keep the motel from looking empty."

Click.

What *was* that noise? I had to find out. I carefully put my bowl on the floor and turned so I could peek around the door frame. I was level with the back of Pa's knees and could see the mess of papers he had behind the counter. The lady had turned and was staring out the side window. When I looked up, I could see the ends of those long fingernails of hers. They were picking at the Formica that had come unglued where the chip was. I don't even think she knew she was doing it. I swung back out of sight before they caught me sitting there.

"I sleep most of the day, so I won't be a bother, and I'm over at Harry's Cabaret in the evenings," she said.

"Well . . ." I could hear Pa was coming around. I couldn't believe it! He was thinking about letting some stranger actually *live* in my motel. How could he do that to me? She'd always be around, interfering with everything I did. Pa and Ruby and me, we did just fine on our own. We didn't need anybody else in there messing things up. Who was this lady anyway? And why did she sleep all day? Talk about lazy! She must be the laziest person in the world.

The clicking stopped while Pa pondered. I sat still as could be.

"We'll give it a try for a month," Pa finally said. "You can have Room 4."

The lady sighed like she had been holding her breath and then made a funny noise. I thought she was going to cry.

"Thank you," she said.

I heard Pa start to move behind the counter, so I jumped up and rushed into the kitchen with my empty bowl. I was sitting at the table, licking my spoon and staring at the school papers when Pa walked in.

"Evangeline," he said. "Mary Ann will be staying for a month in Room 4. Here are the keys. Take her to her room, will you? Jesse's on his way over."

"But—" I didn't want to do it, but I knew that when Jesse

and his cold beer were coming, there was no use arguing. Pa had his mind set. "OK, Pa," I said. Maybe I could find out what this lady was up to.

She picked up the two suitcases and walked along the row of rooms with me, balancing just fine on those tall high heels.

"So what do they call you?" she asked.

I thought about not saying anything, but Pa had taught me to be polite to customers, so I had to answer. "Eddie," I said.

"Hi, Eddie. I'm Angelique."

"But Pa just called you Mary Ann," I couldn't help reminding her.

"Everybody calls me Angelique because my stage name is Angelique Starr. That's Starr—with two Rs."

"Are you an actress?"

"I work nights over at Harry's Cabaret—you know, the gentlemen's club in that pink building over on Harmony Road?"

I nodded. I'd seen the building. I pulled her room key out of my pocket. "I never knew anybody named Angelique before."

"Angelique means 'angelic' in French," she said as we opened the door to Room 4. "I just love angels."

When she dropped the suitcases in the middle of the floor, her hair came unpinned and fell into a ponytail. She shook her head, making the ponytail bounce. With her hair down, she didn't seem very old at all. I watched her check out the room, taking in the paneling on the walls; the green- and gold-flowered bedspread that matched the curtains in the windows; and the television in the corner on a little table. She smiled. I'd hoped she'd hate it and go away and leave me and Pa and Ruby alone, but I think she liked her motel room.

"This is the first place I've had that's all my own," she said. She ran her fingers over the spread and then flopped onto her back in the middle of the bed. "You can come visit me after school if you want." She turned over onto her side. "I can show you how to put on makeup and fix your hair pretty. Do you think your pa would mind if I put up a few decorations?"

"I guess not," I said as I went out the door. "Just don't mess things up."

How should I know what Pa would say? I'd have bet a million dollars he wouldn't have let somebody actually live in our motel, and I'd have been dead wrong. I felt some worry inside my chest. Between him and Miss Rose, nothing was the same. I wasn't sure about anything anymore. I did know one thing, though. Forget about putting makeup on me and fixing my hair. I sure didn't need any of *that* kind of fussing.

CHAPTER 8

Now that I was sitting in the front of the classroom, Miss Rose saw everything I did. I couldn't look out the window or bring out a book to read when things got boring. She even took away a picture I was drawing while she was going over a math problem for the third time. I understood it right away and couldn't believe the other kids in the class were really that stupid.

Every once in a while, I'd look back at my old seat at the other end of the room. I truly wished I could go back there to stay, but it wasn't my desk anymore—Carol Anne Williams was sitting there. It did my heart some good, though, to see that she hated it.

Carol Anne picked the front row every year, and the teachers thought she was the greatest thing there was. She always did her homework and raised her hand so much it's a wonder it didn't cramp up. She wore blouses instead of T-shirts and carried this silly little purse wherever she went. It was a mystery to me what she kept in it. Nothing much, I guessed, except her brush. She was always brushing her hair—in the class, in the bathroom, on the playground, everywhere. It was disgusting.

I could tell Farrell didn't like sitting near the front, either. He mostly slouched down in his chair and tapped his pencil on the desk. I knew he drew pictures, too, but Miss Rose never caught him at it because I blocked her view. It wasn't fair.

Even though my back was to Farrell most of the time, I did sense a change in him every time the hall got noisy and Miss Rose closed the classroom door. As soon as it clicked shut, he would stiffen and sit real still. I knew he didn't like it closed at all. Maybe it was because of where they sent him after his mama died. I figured he had to work it out for himself, though. If Miss Rose thought the door should be shut, she'd shut it. I sure wasn't going to tell her or anybody else his secret.

It turned out I didn't have to. The kids found out anyway, the day Miss Rose needed some more chalk from the supply closet. The piece she was using was so little I was afraid her fingernails were going to scrape on the board and set my teeth to tingling.

"Farrell?" she said, turning away from the board and wiping her hands on the sides of her dress. "You're so nice and tall. Would you please get me a new box of chalk from the supply closet?"

Farrell didn't answer so I turned around. He sat there frozen, acting like he didn't hear her.

"Farrell? It's on the top shelf in the back. Green box."

Farrell looked up at her and then got up and walked slowly to the back of the classroom. The other kids started working again, but I kept watching him. He got to the supply closet door and opened it, but he didn't go right in. He waited for a minute. I guess he was looking for the chalk. Then he kind of took a deep breath and marched in.

There was some breeze that day, and we had the windows open, so maybe that's what made the door close. Nobody else noticed, but I saw the door start to move, faster and faster, until it clicked shut on Farrell. One second later he blasted out of the closet, slamming the door open so hard it banged against the wall. Everybody jumped and turned to look at him.

He was quite a sight, too, standing by the door. His eyes were all bugged out so I could see the whites all around—like a picture I saw of a horse that was scared. He was breathing hard and shaking, like there'd been a ghost in there with him. The kids started to giggle. Farrell just stood there staring straight ahead, the upside-down box of chalk squeezed tight in his hand.

Miss Rose hurried back to where he was. "Farrell? What happened?"

Farrell didn't answer. He didn't move a muscle.

Miss Rose put her hand on his shoulder, and that broke the spell.

"Here," he said, shoving the box of chalk out toward her.

When he did that, the lid popped open, and chalk went flying everywhere. The kids were still giggling some from before, and they started laughing so hard at Farrell that everybody in the rest of the school probably heard.

Miss Rose's eyes took in the whole class. "Hush, children. All of you go back to work." The kids got quiet and bent over their papers. I knew they were still laughing, though. I couldn't see their faces, but their shoulders were shaking.

Farrell got down on his hands and knees. He picked up the pieces and stuffed them back into the box.

"Here," he said, handing it to Miss Rose and going back to his seat. He didn't look at me. I turned back around to face front. I knew this was something the kids were never going to forget.

CHAPTER 9

One afternoon not too long after school started, Miss Rose stood in front of the class with a stack of papers in her arms.

"I'm going to give you a couple of tests to see where you all stand," she said as she began passing them out. "This first one is an aptitude test. It will tell me what each of you is capable of. The second one is an achievement test. It will tell me how much you know about what you've been taught so I can make up a study plan for the year."

Soon the room was quiet with concentration. I thought the two tests were fun. The first one was a breeze. The second one was much harder, but I still knew most of the answers.

I was the first one finished. I looked around, and everybody else was still working. I could hear pencils scratching on the paper and kids sighing. I figured I must have done something wrong since I was the only one done. I picked up my pencil again and frowned at my paper like everyone else was doing. I let out a big sigh for good measure. Then I checked my answers another time. I couldn't find anything to change, so I tried to look like I was thinking real hard. Farrell started poking me in the back with his pencil. I guessed he was finished, too.

Finally Carol Anne got up and sashayed past me to put her tests on the teacher's desk. When she turned to go back to her seat, she had this silly, smug grin on her face, like somebody should congratulate her for being first.

After a few more kids took their tests up to the front, I decided to make my move. Farrell was right behind me. Miss Rose smiled up at us both. She really had a nice smile. Too bad she was such a thorn in my life.

When she gave the tests back a few days later, Miss Rose was absolutely beaming.

"Class," she said. "You did very well on the tests. I'll use them this year to get to know all of you better." I really wished she'd quit trying to get to know me better, but there was no stopping that woman.

"Two of you even scored ninety-five, the highest in the class! Now," she warned, "these scores are not to be shared with each other. You're to take them home to your parents and to keep them for your own information. You'll find your scores written on the back page. Remember, they're just for *your* eyes."

With that, she started passing out the tests. Finally mine

flopped down on my desk. The other kids were whispering, and papers were rattling as they checked out their scores. Nobody talked to me or Farrell, but that's the way they always were.

I waited a minute and then peeked at the last page. It had "95" written in red. I put the papers back together and had to try real hard to keep a little smile from tickling at the corners of my mouth. I had one of the highest scores in the class! One of two. I wondered who the other person was. I hoped it was Farrell.

I allowed myself to turn around just a little to catch Farrell's eye, but he was pretending to study his test and wouldn't look up. Then I knew who got the other 95. One glance at Carol Anne, and I was sure it was her. She had a grin on her face so big that if she wasn't careful, her teeth would fall out. Of all the kids, it had to be her. Miss Rose had said not to tell, but most of them couldn't keep their mouths shut if their lives depended on it. Pretty soon everybody would know Carol Anne got one of the 95s. But I wasn't going to tell anyone my score, especially not Carol Anne. I wasn't in her little fan club and it would drive her crazy not knowing. I found that thought very satisfying. I folded up my test and stuck it in my notebook.

I usually didn't share stuff with Pa. He was busy and mostly didn't seem to care. But that day I could hardly wait to get home to tell him. I was finally first in something, and it was hard to keep the happiness inside.

When school was over, I didn't even wait for Farrell. I

just kind of floated down the street toward home. The sky was bluer than I had ever seen it, and the little tufts of grass along the way had to be the world's greenest green. I even smiled and waved to Gus, who I didn't usually like, as he arranged stuff in the window of his pawnshop. I couldn't help it. It was a good day, and I had happiness bubbles inside.

I hurried through the office and behind the counter to the doorway of our little apartment.

Some game show was on, and the audience was cheering and clapping.

"Pa!" I called over the racket of the television. At first there was no answer. Then I heard a noise from the couch. Holding my test papers tight in my hand, I walked across the room. Pa was stretched out on the couch. He looked like he was asleep, but I knew in a second, from all the other times, that he wasn't just sleeping. He was off in that never-never land brought on by Jesse's beer and whiskey. The TV tray next to him was full of empty beer cans, and they were scattered on the floor around it.

"Pa!" I called again.

Pa snorted and scratched his chest but never opened his eyes. Instead, he turned over and started snoring.

"Pa!" It came out in a whisper because all of a sudden I couldn't swallow, my throat was aching so.

I looked down at the test papers I was holding, the ones I had been so proud of, and then back at Pa lying there. He was like a big, snoring lump. I felt a terrible, desperate anger boiling in my body. I hated Pa right then, hated him with all my might. Hated his dirty old-man kind of undershirts and his ratty blue jeans. Hated his snoring and especially hated those beer cans. I wanted to throw them all through the television screen.

Instead, I threw the tests as far as I could across the room and turned to get the hell out of there. I ran right into Farrell, who was standing behind me holding his basketball. I hadn't heard him come in.

"Get out of my way," I said, giving him a shove.

He had to step backward to catch his balance and dropped the ball. I heard it roll toward the kitchen and bump into the table. He grabbed my wrist as I pushed past.

"Wait," he said.

"No!" I twisted away from him, but he held tight and grabbed my other wrist.

I tried to tell him to leave me alone, but nothing came out. My throat hurt so much it felt like I couldn't get enough air, and tears were stinging my eyes. I looked away so he wouldn't notice, but he turned me around to face him. He was more serious than I'd ever seen him.

"Eddie," he said quietly, his eyes on mine while he gestured with his head toward Pa, "you're forgetting about my daddy. I know how it is."

When he said that, it was like all the fight drained out of me. I couldn't stop the tears anymore. They ran in wet trickles down my cheeks and into the neck of my T-shirt. Farrell let go of my wrists and stood there for a minute. Then he put his arms around me. He patted my back while I leaned against him, making damp circles on his T shirt.

"I'm sorry," I said as I got control and wiped my eyes. "I'm OK now."

He backed away and looked like he wasn't sure what to do. "Want to shoot some baskets?" he asked.

I nodded, even though I didn't want anybody on the street to see me with red eyes. Eddie Brown wasn't a crybaby.

I guess Farrell understood what I was thinking. He reached into the Lost and Found box behind the counter and pulled out a pair of sunglasses. "Here," he said. "Put these on. We'll put 'em back later. The sun's really bright today."

We walked out of the cool motel office and into the heat of the Florida afternoon.

Farrell didn't say anything all the way to the school yard, and I was grateful for that. My mood was recovering, and I was plotting my newest basketball moves when he turned to me.

"You got the highest score on the tests, didn't you?" he asked as we went through the open gate.

"Me and Carol Anne," I said, disgusted.

"Well, I didn't. And I've been thinking on it. I'm ready to make you a deal. I'll teach you to fight like a boy—not just a few pointers, but really teach you proper, with lessons and all—if you'll help me with my schoolwork sometimes. Course, it has to stay between us."

I gave him a sharp look to see if he was teasing. He didn't

have to worry about me telling anyone. I wasn't exactly overflowing with friends, and he knew it. He tossed the ball up and down while I pondered it some.

"OK, it's a deal," I said. It might keep me from stewing so much about Miss Rose's visit. Besides, the way things were going in my life, I figured I just might need to know how to fight.

CHAPTER 10

"Meet me behind the motel," Farrell said the next afternoon after school. It was time for my first fighting lesson, and I felt some excitement in my gut. But then Farrell spoiled it. As he got ready to head for Jesse's garage to leave off his books and grab a snack, he stopped and looked me up and down the way a pa would look at a little kid. "Better change out of your school clothes, too," he added as he started to walk away.

Now that was taking this teaching stuff too far. Who did he think he was, telling me what to wear? He wasn't my pa, and I wasn't some little kid. He couldn't tell me what to do.

I spun around and stomped into the motel without saying a word to make my point. Oh, I'd change my clothes, all right. I smiled a secret smile as I put on my oldest jeans and T-shirt. My plan was to catch him by surprise. I figured I'd have him flat on the ground in no time, and if I had to get good and grubby doing it, well, it would be worth it to show him he couldn't boss me around.

I was going into the motel's little backyard when Farrell caught up with me.

"It's mostly dirt back here," he said, pointing to two lonely clumps of grass, "but it'll do."

I nodded, keeping my face straight, but I was laughing at him on the inside. I couldn't help remembering the last time we were in the yard, when we'd run away from Jesse, and Farrell'd looked just like a raccoon because of the garage oil smeared all over his face.

"OK, what do I do?" I asked as he moved away from me. I was ready to teach him a lesson.

Farrell bent his knees a little and faced me. "Go ahead and hit me," he said, shifting slowly from one foot to the other and motioning to me with his hands. "Take a punch."

"Where?"

"Anywhere."

He looked like an easy target just standing there. I couldn't wait to slam him to the ground. He'd think twice about bossing me around again, that's for sure. I bided my time, then suddenly stepped up and swung at him. He blocked my arm and reached out and shoved me right over, easy as can be. I landed hard on my butt, and my teeth rattled. I couldn't believe how easy he'd put me down. I hadn't even come close. Farrell moved in front of me, his shadow blocking the sun.

"How'd you do that?" I asked, looking up from the dirt. I had to know his secret.

Farrell held out his hand and helped me up. I brushed off the seat of my jeans.

"You just gotta know how to stand and where to hit," he said, shrugging. "Look. First you got to remember to keep your head down. And keep your fists up close to your face to protect yourself."

I raised my fists in front of my face. I felt like a boxer on TV and wondered how they could see what they were doing.

"Not that high." Farrell pushed my hands down a little, and I could see his face all the way to his chin. Then he took my right fist and opened it up. "Don't stick your thumb down inside like that. You could break it easy if you punch somebody." I closed my hands into fists again, but with the thumbs on the outside. "OK, now come at me again, but this time in slow motion."

I swung slowly at him, bringing my fist from way back for extra punch. He flicked my arms away.

"You're fighting like a girl," he said.

That did it. "I *am* a girl!" I wanted to haul off and slug him, knock him to the ground, make him yell for mercy, but it came to me that I really didn't know how to do that. I needed to learn to fight the right way, and, I hated to admit it, I needed Farrell to teach me.

I took a deep breath. "OK, show me," I said.

Me and Farrell met every afternoon after school to practice our fighting.

"Bend your knees. . . . Keep your feet apart. . . . Put one foot a little in front of the other for balance. . . . Hold your hands close in front of your face to protect it. . . . Punch straight forward, and bring your fist back quick. . . ."

Farrell was a good teacher. I was starting to feel like I could hold my own against any kid in the class.

One afternoon after we finished our lesson, we sat in the shade of the motel trying to cool off. Our legs were stretched out in front of us, and we leaned our backs against the wall.

"You're doing good," Farrell said. "You could probably fight kids bigger than you now and win, too. I like to win." His hand fiddled with the grass clump next to his leg. "I got into this fight at one school I went to. Beat up a kid. Worst bully around. Guess I showed him a thing or two." He grinned at the memory.

"Did Jesse teach you to fight?"

Farrell yanked out a piece of grass and folded it between his fingers. "Nope. I just watched the other kids and learned on my own." He hesitated for a second. "I *had* to learn. You got to know how to fight when you live in foster homes and go to a bunch of different schools."

I stopped watching the grass he was holding and looked over at him. "Foster homes?"

"That's where Social Services sends you to live with different families. Some of the ones I went to were nice, but other ones had nasty kids in them. That's why I learned to fight. I wasn't always big like I am now, and those other kids liked to beat up on anybody smaller than them. I had to protect myself."

I wasn't sure what to think. I didn't know about foster homes and people sending kids to live with people who weren't their kin. But I did know about nasty kids, that's for sure.

Farrell continued to wrinkle the piece of grass. "I ran away a couple of times, too." He sounded boastful as he looked over at me, and the corners of his mouth flickered in the tiniest smile. "Fighting and running away. I've done them both. I can do them again if I need to."

He leaned his head against the wall and closed his eyes. Neither of us said anything for a few minutes. Farrell looked like he was resting, but my mind was going a mile a minute. I never knew about Farrell living in foster houses. I just thought him and Jesse moved around a lot. But why would Jesse let him be sent to live with people he didn't know?

"Farrell?" It came out in a whisper. "Why did Social Services send you away?"

Farrell slowly brought his head away from the wall and opened his eyes. The little smile was gone from his face, and he threw the piece of grass onto the dirt.

"Look. Can't we just stick to fighting lessons?" he asked. "I don't want to talk about it right now."

I opened my mouth to say something, but he pushed himself up and got ready to walk away. "Not today. OK?"

"Sure," I said, getting up to follow him. But I didn't really mean it. I wanted to know.

CHAPTER 11

Not too long after that, Miss Rose made me and Farrell project partners for a school report. I didn't like having a project partner, even if it was Farrell, because then we both had to go to the library to look things up. I liked going there on my own. I felt like it was my very own special place, and Mrs. Jenkins, the librarian, was my very own special person. She always knew which were the good books, and called me Miss Brown, just like I was a grown-up.

Mrs. Jenkins had gray hair and wore long skirts and brown rubber shoes so she didn't make any noise when she walked. She could sneak up on anybody who wasn't behaving and scare the daylights out of them. I liked to watch her do that. It served them right for making noise.

And I could just smell all the learning that went on in that building. It was so cool and quiet and peaceful, I couldn't even hear the traffic going up and down the street outside. And Mrs. Jenkins always let me stay as long as I wanted.

But after Miss Rose gave us the assignment, I decided I owed it to Farrell to take him there. He was teaching me to fight proper-like, just the way he'd promised. I figured it was only right I should help him with his school stuff the way I'd promised.

So one afternoon me and Farrell took our notebooks and walked to the library. The big wooden doors were heavy, but it was a grand building, and I felt important going into its cool darkness.

Mrs. Jenkins was sitting at her desk reading some papers. She was wearing a pretty gray blouse and some little silver earrings. She looked over her glasses to see who we were.

"Good afternoon, Miss Brown," she said to us with a nod and a smile as we walked up to her desk. Her voice was so quiet and restful, all the anxiousness went right out of me. I smiled right back.

"This here's Farrell Garrett," I said, pointing to Farrell, who stood next to me. "We're working on a report for school and need to look some stuff up."

"What is your report about?"

I couldn't help but sigh at the boring subject Farrell had picked from the list Miss Rose had on the blackboard. "We need to find out about phosphate mining. Miss Rose said it turns into fertilizer."

"I know just the books. Come along with me, and I'll show you."

She stood up and walked across the room in those quiet shoes of hers. We went right after her, but we weren't nearly as quiet.

She pointed to the books on the shelf. "These are the best books," she said. "Let me know if you need any help. I'll be right over there."

Farrell was smiling when we sat down at one of the big wooden tables. I guess Mrs. Jenkins got to him, too, and I decided I really didn't mind so much sharing her with him.

We each picked out a couple of books, and mine were so heavy they banged when they hit the table. A lady in a blue dress who was putting books back on the shelves frowned at us, and we couldn't help but grin a little. We tried to be quieter as we opened our notebooks and pulled out some paper.

"Look at this," I said, pointing to a picture in one of the books in my stack. It was of some machinery around a big hole. "It says Florida has more phosphate mining than any-place in the country."

"Yeah," said Farrell, thumbing through one of the books. "I already know that."

"You do not."

"I do so."

"Not."

"Look, Eddie, I know a lot of that stuff. That's why I picked it for us to write about." He stopped turning the pages.

"OK, if you're so smart, how do you know it?"

Farrell sighed. "Remember when I told you I lived in some foster homes? Well, that's how I know. In one of the houses the father worked at a phosphate mine near town. It looked just like the one in that picture." He pointed to the page in the open book. "Yep. That's just the way it looked. That was the last family I went to before Daddy came and got me this time, and we moved to Paradise. The other kids there were pretty nice to me. Not like the ones in the first house where I lived. I went to the first one when I was really little, right after my ma died."

Farrell shivered, even though it wasn't that cold in the library. I held my breath, afraid he would stop talking.

"In the first foster place they sent me, the big kids who were already there thought it would be funny to get me to climb into the big toy box. I was little and thought they were playing with me. But when I got in, they closed the lid and sat on it." He was whispering so low I could hardly hear him. "I yelled and banged, but they just laughed. It was dark inside and I was scared, and I couldn't get out. After a while they ran off."

"Is that why you don't like to be closed in?"

Farrell blinked like he was just waking up. "I don't know. Maybe. I don't like it when I'm closed in someplace and can't get away. I guess maybe it is."

He picked up the book and started turning the pages, and I knew he was through talking.

Two days later, me and Farrell finished up our report at the kitchen table in the motel. We had cold sodas in front of us, and we'd swiped a bag of chips from the display stand near the front counter.

"We going to turn this in tomorrow?" he asked.

I looked at him over the papers and books spread out in front of us. We were partners. It wouldn't be right making him look bad just because I didn't care about handing in my homework.

I bit my lip. "I guess so," I said with a sigh, closing the rest of the books and stacking them neatly.

School had become such a trial. Miss Rose had taken to calling on me for answers even if I didn't raise my hand, which I never did. It was like she always had her eye on me there in the front row. But she couldn't make me do my homework. I'd never turned it in before and still didn't. First of all, I already knew most of the stuff. Second, I just didn't feel like it. Pa never asked, and Ruby was always gone in the evenings. I didn't want to give Miss Rose the satisfaction.

"Here," I said, shoving the report across the table to Farrell. "*You* hand it in."

CHAPTER 12

A couple of days later, Miss Rose stopped by my desk at the end of school. "Eddie, will you stay after for a few minutes?" she asked when the last bell rang.

"Sure," I said, just as if I stayed after every day for a chat. But I was scared that she was going to tell me it was time for her home visit to Pa—to get to know us better. Thinking about it kept me awake some at night, but I still hadn't worked out how to keep her away. Then I remembered she hadn't been to Farrell's house yet, and "Garrett" came before "Brown" in the backward-alphabet way she was doing it.

The other kids made a lot of noise as they picked up their papers. I saw a couple of them looking at me and Farrell and whispering together in the corner before they hurried out. Farrell went on past them like they weren't even there. After I put my books in my backpack, Miss Rose leaned across her desk toward me.

"I just wanted to tell you something," she said. "The report you and Farrell wrote was excellent. I know you spent a lot of time on it, and I wanted to let you know it showed. You do very good work."

I tried not to show it, but her words made me happy, and I was grinning from ear to ear on the inside. But then she spoiled it when she said, "I just wish you would apply yourself like that more often. I know you can do better if you just try."

I'd heard that kind of talk all my life. I was sick of hearing it. Did she think she was the first one to come up with that? Of course I could do better if I tried. I just didn't want to try—in this class or any class.

"Yes, Miss Rose," I said, holding my books tight to me. I could feel my mouth stiffen as I turned to leave. I felt like kicking something.

Forget it, Farrell, I thought. I'm not going to write any more reports with you or anyone else. Nobody is going to expect me to do things I might not be able to do next time. I won't do it. Not anymore.

When I closed the classroom door behind me, I heard a noise echoing from down the hall that made me forget to breathe.

"Let me out! Hey! Let me out of here!" It was Farrell! It sounded like he was banging hard on something. His shouting was kind of muffled, but I could hear enough to know his voice was high and tight, pretty near hysterical.

I dropped my schoolbooks on the floor and rushed down the empty hall and around the corner. Four or five kids were holding the janitor's closet door closed. Without even thinking about it, I ran at them with my head down and knocked them over like bowling pins. With the kids out of the way, Farrell pushed the closet door open, jumped out, and joined in the ruckus. We punched and kicked just like we'd practiced. Those stupid kids didn't stand a chance. Pretty soon *they* were the ones yelling, and I could hear teachers coming out of their empty classrooms and running toward us.

Carol Anne had been standing to the side egging everybody on, and I finally couldn't take it anymore. I had Brian Yorkey pinned to the floor, but I reached out, grabbed her by her ankles, and jerked her feet out from under her. She came toppling down on top of everyone, skinning her elbows and messing up that perfect hair she was always brushing.

By now the teachers were running up to the tangle of kids and pulling us apart. "Stop it! Stop it this instant!"

It didn't take long for them to separate everybody. Mrs. Higgins held my arms behind my back, and Mr. Amos had an armlock on Farrell. The rest of the kids had been grabbed tight by other teachers. Everybody was talking at once. Mr. Amos whistled loud through his teeth, and the sound about pierced my eardrum. It must have bounced off the walls and shot clear out the back of the building. The hall was quiet for about two seconds. Then all the teachers started talking at once.

"What is going on?"

"What were you all thinking of?"

"You know there is no fighting in school."

"This isn't the way you were taught."

The kids pointed at Farrell and me. "Eddie and Farrell, they started it."

And Carol Anne whined, "She knocked me down, and I banged my elbows. I need a Band-Aid. I'm bleeding."

Me and Farrell just stood there, real quiet-like. We weren't about to give them the satisfaction of hearing us say anything. But I noticed that Joey Johnson had a bloody nose, and Bradley Richards was picking the buttons of his shirt up off the floor. Carol Anne's hair was sticking up in the back like an Indian headdress. I let my foot slip over to nudge Farrell's so he would see. His tiny smile told me he hadn't missed a thing.

The upshot of it was that me and Farrell got suspended for two days, but so did everybody else in the hallway that afternoon. Anyone fighting on school grounds was automatically suspended for two days—county rule. It didn't matter who started it or anything.

That was fine with Farrell and me. We had two days off to stay home and do what we wanted. I didn't get it myself. Get into trouble, get a vacation. Maybe the other kids were punished when they got home, but when I gave the note to Pa, who'd already had a couple of beers, he just asked if we'd won. I figured we did because they sure looked a lot worse than we did when it was over. Jesse was sitting next to Pa on a metal chair outside the motel office at the time.

"Four or five against two ain't fair," he said, wiping his hands on his greasy coveralls and looking us up and down.

Pa nodded. "Maybe they'll leave you alone now."

I wasn't sure what Pa meant by that because neither one of them ever asked what the fight was about. He was right, though; nobody at school messed with us again.

Pa sipped his beer. "You both have to stay at the motel or the garage for the next two days. Can't have them finding you wandering the streets if you're suspended."

"Yes, Pa."

"Farrell, you'll help out in the garage," Jesse said. "There's plenty to do, and the tools need cleaning."

Farrell nodded.

With that, me and Farrell hurried on into the motel office before they could think of anything else for us to do. We had two days off! Two days of vacation in the middle of school. Not bad for scuffling with some kids who should've been straightened out a long time ago.

CHAPTER 13

The next day Angelique came out of her room as I carried a load of sheets and towels to dump in the hamper. Me and Ruby were almost finished cleaning the rooms after lunch.

"Hi, Eddie," she said with a wave of her long fingernails. I didn't get to see her much, just sometimes in the evening when she was on her way out, dressed in her spiky shoes and fancy clothes. I guess she acted in a lot of plays at Harry's Cabaret because she went there almost every night.

Angelique usually gave me a wave when she spotted me, and I'd wave back. At first I did it because she was a paying customer. After a while, though, I waved back because I wanted to, I guess mostly because she'd kept to herself and hadn't messed with my life like I'd been afraid she would. She even cleaned her own room; that must have been part of Pa's deal. Fact was, I hadn't been in it since I took her and her two suitcases there the day she came to stay.

I dropped the towels in the hamper.

"How're you doing?" I asked her as I rolled the cart toward the office. I decided Ruby could take them to the Laundromat and do the rest on her own this time.

"Come and sit," Angelique said, pulling over the rusty metal chair from in front of the room next door to hers. "Want a soda?"

"Sure do." I pushed my damp hair away from my forehead. It might have been fall, but Florida doesn't cool off till about November, and it was hotter than blazes.

She came back out of her room with a soda for each of us and popped mine for me before she handed me the can. I thought that was real nice of her.

We both took a sip and sighed at the joy of it. She leaned back and closed her eyes. I tried not to stare at her because it wasn't polite, but I studied her out of the corner of my eye, acting like I was looking up and down the street. She sure looked different without all that makeup. In fact, she looked really young. Her hair was pulled back in a ponytail, and she had on white shorts and a yellow tank top. She was barefoot, and I couldn't miss that her toenails matched her fingernails. I never could understand why people painted their toenails. Feet are ugly to begin with. Why paint them and draw attention?

"I have this idea," Angelique said, turning to me. Real

quick, I looked up from her feet. "Just look at these chairs." She rubbed her hands along the arms of the one she was sitting in.

I looked. They were the same green metal chairs that always sat outside the rooms. The backs kind of fanned out like seashells. There were only two front legs that bent down one side, around the back, and up the other side. That made the chairs springy. I wasn't heavy enough to make them bounce, but old Mr. Dossey could. He used to stay with us when his truck came through and weighed about five hundred pounds. I was sure his chair would bust in half every time he sat down. I was afraid we'd have to pick him up off the ground if it did, and I wasn't sure how we'd ever do that. It never happened, though. Maybe that's why the chairs were still there outside the motel rooms. They were indestructible. And ugly, too. I'd never noticed before.

"I'm going to paint the one outside my room," Angelique said. "Just look at the rust and the dirt on it. It'll ruin my clothes, and I can't stand that gosh-awful green color."

"What color will you paint it?"

"White. Pure, bright, clean white. If I'm going to live here, I'm not going to live in a dump." She hesitated. "No offense," she added.

I nodded. "If you have an extra brush, I'll help you . . . if you want, that is. I'm finished helping Ruby, and Farrell won't be done at the garage till after supper."

She gave me the prettiest smile and went inside to get the paint.

So we cleaned and painted and chatted, just like two lady friends. I was curious about something and decided it wasn't really prying to ask.

"How come you don't use the name Mary Ann? Don't you like it?"

She rolled her eyes and her cheeks dimpled. "I like Angelique Starr better. Don't you think it has more of a ring to it?"

"They're both real pretty names," I said, although I had to admit that Mary Ann sounded right ordinary. But seeing her with her bare feet and white chair paint smeared on her face, she sure looked more like a Mary Ann.

"Angelique is just so . . . I don't know . . . so much more romantic. It sounds like Paris and going places and dancing on warm summer nights under the stars."

She got this dreamy look in her eyes, and I knew that even though she was looking straight at it, she wasn't seeing the traffic and dust and grit of Celestial Avenue.

"We're about finished with the painting here," she said, like she was coming back to earth. She closed the lid on the paint can. "Want to see my room? I decorated it. I hope your Pa doesn't mind, but I can take it all down in a jiffy and put everything back the way it was."

Did I want to see her room? Was she nuts? I'd seen her going in with packages and boxes and had heard hammering sometimes in the afternoon. Sure I wanted to see what she had been up to!

I set my brush on the newspaper and stood up. "I'd like that," I said.

I don't know what I expected. Of course, the room wasn't much to start with, but she was such an elegant person when she went out at night, I guess I thought it would look like something out of a magazine. Like a place a movie star would live.

It took a minute for my eyes to get used to the darkness after the bright sun. Then I saw them. Angels. Angels everywhere. Pictures of angels in frames hanging on the walls. Cardboard ones dangling on strings from the ceiling. Paper ones taped around the mirror. Statue angels sitting on the dresser and on the night table. Even angels pasted to the front of the little refrigerator she'd bought from the pawnshop. I didn't know what to say.

She was watching me and frowned like she was worried. "Do you think your pa will mind?"

I was still looking around.

"I can take it all down. . . ." she said, her voice trailing off. "They'll come down easy. . . ."

"I've never seen so many angels," I said.

She smiled like she was relieved and then got excited, like a kid showing off a new birthday bike or something.

"I cut a lot of them out of magazines. Sometimes I buy them in the discount store, especially the glass ones. I just love angels."

I could sure see that.

"I pretend like they're watching over me. Keeping me safe."

I nodded.

"Now watch this." She closed the curtains tight and

turned out the lights. The ceiling lit up with hundreds and hundreds of glowing green stars.

"I buy them when I get some extra money and stick them up there. They're the glow-in-the-dark kind. It's almost like camping under the stars."

I'd never been camping, so I figured she probably knew what she was talking about.

"I picked Angelique Starr for my stage name because I like angels and stars so much." She almost couldn't hold it in how proud she was of everything. I think it was real important to her that I liked what she had done.

"It's very pretty," I said. And it was . . . in a weird sort of way. Now me, I might get the willies having all those eyes staring at me all the time, but it sure would be a comfort to have hundreds of angels watching over me, too. Then I could relax and quit looking out for myself so much.

"It looks like a fairyland," I said truthfully. "You did a real nice job."

She beamed. "Come back again," she said as I started to leave. "I'll show you how to fix your hair up pretty, and I'll bet you'd look a lot older with a little makeup on."

"Thanks," I said. I didn't want to hurt her feelings, but there was no way she was going to play beauty shop with me. I was sure of it—100 percent positive.

CHAPTER 14

About a week later, Miss Rose walked over and stood in front of my desk. I was trying to copy a math problem from the blackboard, and she was right in my way. "Eddie? Can you usually see the board clearly?"

It was like she thought up something new to bother me with every day.

"I guess so," I said. "Yeah, I can see it fine." I could see it better if you would get out of my way, I thought, but I didn't say it.

"I've noticed that you're squinting a lot lately."

"Things are clearer here than they were in the back," I answered, and then I could have bit my tongue. If I wasn't careful, she'd think I liked it up there in the front and never let me go back to my old desk.

When the last bell rang and I was leaving, Miss Rose

handed me a note to give to Pa. I waited until I was outside to read it.

I have noticed that Eddie seems to have difficulty seeing the blackboard in class, the note said. *I suggest she have her eyes tested. She may need glasses.*

My eyes tested? Glasses? It seemed like Miss Rose just couldn't leave me alone. I was half-tempted to toss the note in the trash and sit in class with my eyes propped wide open, but I knew I'd never hear the end of it if I didn't bring the note to Pa.

Jesse must have been low on beer money because when I got home, Pa was awake and sitting on the metal chair in front of the office, soaking up the afternoon sun. Sometimes it was better if he was a little bit drunk because then he didn't mess with what I was doing—he mostly either ignored me or forgot what I told him. But when I got home that day, there he was, wide awake and waiting.

I handed him the note.

"This true?" he asked. "Are you having trouble seeing the board?"

Now I'd never lie to Pa—he taught me that. "I can see it pretty good. Sometimes small things are a little blurry, but I'm in the front now. I'm doing just fine."

I could tell right away I wasn't going to get off that easy.

"I have a little extra money," he said, jerking his head toward the cash box inside. "Ask Ruby to take you to get your eyes checked as soon as she can."

I started to object but knew it wouldn't do any good. Pa had made up his mind.

So a few days later, me and Ruby got on the bus to go to the fancy end of town. She always let me sit next to the window. I liked riding up so high. It gave me a view of things I couldn't see when I walked, and took me to new places besides.

As we got farther away from the motel, there weren't as many boarded-up buildings. The stores were nicer, and there wasn't hardly any trash and weeds along the road. The houses were farther apart, too, and they were clean and neat. Everything looked like it had new paint on it. I wondered what kind of people lived in those houses. They probably got their clothes at a big, classy store instead of a place like Tina's Thrift Shop. I decided I wouldn't want to live there, though, because I knew they were all like Carol Anne and Janet Abrams, and I didn't want to be like them, that's for sure.

The eye doctor place had soft blue carpet and blue chairs to match. Very elegant.

"I'll wait for you here," Ruby said, slowly lowering herself into one of the chairs and picking up a magazine from the table in front of her. She was really stuffed into that pretty blue chair, and I wondered if she would get stuck in it when it was time to leave.

A lady took me into a room that had most of the lights turned off. She told me to sit in a big leather chair that looked like a dentist's chair. The back of my legs stuck to it, and I wished I'd worn jeans instead of shorts.

The doctor came in right off and checked my eyes. It wasn't long before he scribbled something on a tablet. I knew it. I needed glasses. We went back out to Ruby.

"You can pick out frames now," he told her. "It should take about a week for the glasses to be ready."

Ruby put down her magazine and leaned on the arms of the chair when she got up. I half expected it to pop like a suction cup.

We spent some time looking at frames. There was a whole wall of them. Every pair I tried on looked stupid. I didn't look like me at all. I did find one pair that I liked. They were big and black; I thought I looked like an important secretary.

Ruby nudged my shoulder and handed me a red pair with diamonds in the corners. I shook my head. She put them back.

"How about these?" she asked, pushing a blue pair with rainbow-colored stems into my hands. This was not going well. It was the purple ruffled blouse all over again.

"I like the black ones," I said, carefully putting Ruby's circus glasses back on the shelf. Ruby started to reach for them again.

"These are more her size," said a voice behind me. A lady in a white jacket handed me a pair of glasses. They were smaller and not nearly as important-looking as the black ones, but they also weren't as disgusting as the ones Ruby kept finding with her special Ruby ugly-stuff radar.

I tried them on. They didn't look too bad, but I still didn't like them.

"I'll take them," I said, handing them back to her. The lady smiled. Ruby just sighed.

The next week me and Ruby went back on the bus.

"Now hold your head still," the lady in white said as she

put the new glasses over my ears and wiggled them on my nose. She held up a mirror. "What do you think?"

I moved my head from side to side. I looked like some homely kid who spent her whole life with her nose buried in a book and never did anything. I hated them.

Then I turned and looked out the window of the shop. I could feel my breath suck in at the wonder of it all. The trees had millions of tiny leaves that fluttered in the wind. I could see every blade of grass and every petal on the flowers by the curb. I could even see a small bird on the grass across the street. I watched as he flew up into the tree. He was hopping around in the branches, and I could still see him! I could read the sign on the bus that went past and watch the wispy clouds blow across the sky.

I took the glasses off, and everything was fuzzy. Then I put them back on again. Amazing! I tried, but I just couldn't keep the smile inside.

I turned in my chair and picked up the mirror lying on the counter to check out the glasses again. No getting around it, I thought as I moved my head back and forth, I still looked like a dope. But when I saw the big wall full of glasses behind me in the mirror, I decided it could've been worse—I could have been wearing the ones Ruby picked out.

I kept putting the glasses on and taking them off all the way home on the bus, just to see the difference. I wondered what else I had been missing. I guessed I'd give Miss Rose one point for being right this time. But I still wasn't sure what she was up to, and if anybody in school said anything about my glasses, I'd probably have to knock their block off.

CHAPTER 15

Me and Farrell were sitting at our headquarters outside Room 12 enjoying the cool breeze that had finally rolled in. Pa hardly ever used Room 12 because it was all the way at the end, and people didn't like being too far from the office.

"What do you think of my new glasses?" I asked, touching them lightly.

Farrell sighed. "I told you a hundred times. They're fine. Do they make you see better?" I nodded. "Then what's the problem?"

Sometimes he was the most aggravating person on earth. I was ready to slug him.

He looked toward the office. "The chairs look good," he said.

I felt my chest puff up with pride. What with the time I had when I was suspended and the weekend that came right after, me and Angelique had ended up painting all the chairs that sat in front of the rooms. With the white paint, they looked positively beautiful. "They smell nice, too." I sniffed in their clean newness.

Farrell turned to studying the toe of his tennis shoe. "Miss Rose came to my house yesterday afternoon," he said.

Suddenly the good feeling went out of me like somebody let the air out of a balloon. That meant she was at the Gs. Not too many more days, and she would be at the Bs, and *Brown* would be the first B in her backward alphabet. I could hear my heart beating in my ears.

"What happened?" I had to ask.

He shrugged. "Nothing much. They sat at the kitchen table. Daddy had a beer, and Miss Rose had a soda, and they talked about school and the town and other junk. I didn't pay much attention."

I wanted to shake him.

"What do you mean you didn't pay much attention?" I couldn't believe he didn't tell me before. *He* might not care about it, but *I* sure as heck cared about her coming to see where I lived. I didn't want her there at all. Ever. That's how much I cared.

"Go home, Farrell," I said, standing. "I've got some stuff to do."

Farrell looked at me funny-like, but he got up and wandered off toward the garage. I sat back down to do some thinking. No way was I going to get out of that visit; I knew that. I could pretend to be sick, but she'd just come another day. Close as I could tell, Miss Rose never gave up on anything, especially when it came to messing up my life.

I figured she'd already been to see Carol Anne and Joey Johnson and the other kids in the class. They probably lived in nice little houses with green grass and flowers and mothers in aprons baking cookies—the kind of houses I saw from the bus window when me and Ruby went to get my glasses. And what did I have? No mama; a pa who couldn't be trusted to behave, especially in the afternoon; no yard; no flowers; no nothing.

I got up and walked slowly down the row of motel rooms. When I looked close at the chairs along the way, the ones we'd just fixed up, I saw they weren't pretty like I thought. They were just rusty old things with white paint slapped on them. Maybe having glasses wasn't such a good thing after all. Sometimes they made things too clear. I kicked the wall.

Pa was lying on the couch with the TV on, fast asleep, when I got to our apartment. I went into my room and closed the door. What was I going to do? I couldn't let Miss Rose see where I lived.

I lay down on my bed and thought about the motel with its peeling, faded paint and the burned-out bulbs in the arrow sign. I thought of the weeds in front and the stupid pink Cadillac butt sticking out of the wall. I thought of Angelique and her angels, of Ruby and her sausage fingers and legs, of Pa and his beer, and of me in the middle of it all.

I put my face into my pillow and cried.

It was dark when I woke up, but the weariness hadn't left my heart yet. I turned on the little lamp next to my bed and lay on my back with my hands under my head. I could see most of the room my mama had started to turn from a baby's room to a big girl's room before she took sick and died. Nothing had changed since then. The walls were still light pink. The dresser and mirror and night table were white, but if I looked real close, I could still see where she'd painted over the decals of teddy bears because I was getting too big to have them. There was a pretty pink rug on the floor, although it was getting truly dirty by now.

My stuffed animals, mostly teddy bears, were up on the closet shelf because I didn't play with them anymore. The walls were empty when she died, so I'd taped some posters on them that I got for free at a street fair a while ago. The only thing Mama hadn't had time to change was the little lamp on the night table. It had a cute little bear on the bottom holding up a bunch of colored balloons. He was smiling.

I got up and went over to the dresser. I wound up my pink jewelry box and opened the lid. It played "Somewhere Over the Rainbow" while a tiny ballerina popped up and danced in circles on a mirror inside. The music box was a present from my mama when I turned four. Sometimes she would sing along with it, all about wishes and love and dreams coming true. I closed my eyes and tried hard to hear her singing, but it had been a long time, and I couldn't remember the words.

While the music played and the ballerina danced, I reached out and picked up the picture I had tucked in the corner of the dresser mirror. It was one of the only pictures I had of my mama. I took it over to the little bear lamp. I could see Pa and Mama and me when I was a baby, in front of the motel sign. There were flowers along the driveway, and the building looked bright and cheerful. I noticed Pa was smiling. I hadn't thought much about it, but I hardly ever saw him smile anymore. When Mama first died, Pa wasn't like that at all. We used to do things together, and talk and laugh. Me and Pa were kind of like best friends. But then he started drinking, and now it was hard to remember those times. But there he was in the picture, smiling at Mama, who looked so pretty and young with the wind blowing her dress. She held me in one arm, and with the other hand she held on to her skirt. I put the picture back into the edge of the mirror and sighed.

Now *that* was a place I could have Miss Rose visit, and *those* were parents I could be proud of.

CHAPTER 16

On Saturday I helped Ruby clean the rooms. When we finished pulling the sheet over one of the beds, I reached into my jeans pocket.

"Ruby," I said, holding out the photograph from my mirror. "Tell me about this picture. See the flowers in front of the motel? Where did they come from?"

Ruby gave the sheet another tug and straightened up. She smiled, reaching for the picture. "Your mama planted them. She was always trying to make things better. She was the prettiest little thing. Always singing, too. She could sing like a nightingale."

I never heard a nightingale sing, but I'd read in a library book that a Swedish lady named Jenny Lind could sing like a nightingale. That must have been very beautiful because people went all over the world to hear her. She even came to America to sing.

"Your mama liked to have pretty things around her. She planted the flowers. That front area looked so nice. She made your pa paint the office and the apartment, too. He grumbled, but he did it." Ruby stopped working and looked up at the ceiling like she was trying to remember. "She always kept flowers on the front counter and on the table in your apartment. She kept a lacy tablecloth on that table, too. It was like she just brightened a room when she walked into it. She was such a lady and your pa's true love. He was always grinning like the cat that ate the canary."

Ruby handed the picture back to me and frowned at the bed. "Now hand me that bedspread. It's getting late, and little Magnolia isn't feeling too good. Poor puppy. I think it was the table scraps I fed her last night."

"Eddie," Miss Rose said to me a few days later when school was over. "Would you take this note home to your father? It's about my home visit. I'm looking forward to meeting him."

I took the note from her like it was poison and rushed out the door. As soon as I was out of sight, I opened it. Two days! She was coming in two days! I had two days to . . . to . . . to what? I felt like throwing up. I leaned against a tree and closed my eyes to shut out the thought.

That's where Farrell found me.

"You coming home or what?" he asked, giving me a poke in the arm. I wasn't sure how long he'd been standing there, but for some reason, his poke really annoyed me. I hit him with my fist.

"What's eating you?" Farrell asked.

"Miss Rose is coming day after tomorrow to visit Pa, and I don't know what to do."

"Do about what?"

"About her coming to the motel, that's what."

"I told you it was no big deal."

"Well, it is to me. I want things to be nice, and I don't know how to do it."

He shifted his books to the other arm. "You'll do just fine. You always do. Look. You think on it some. While you do that, I'm going to shoot some baskets before I go home. Then I have to help my daddy in the garage."

"Wait," I said grabbing the back of his shirt as he started to walk away. "You've got to keep Jesse away from my pa day after tomorrow."

"Why?"

Honestly, sometimes I wondered if that boy wasn't just plain stupid.

"I don't want Pa drinking before Miss Rose comes by. You tell Jesse to stay away and keep his beer and whiskey away, too."

"I'll try," Farrell said, "but I don't know how much good it will do. You know my daddy . . . and your pa, too."

I surely did, and he didn't need to remind me.

"That all?"

"Yep. See ya," I said, still annoyed with the way he acted. How could he let Miss Rose come to his house, looking the way it did, and not care? I'd been in it a few times, and it was a real pigsty, though I can't say it was all their fault.

Farrell and Jesse lived in a little gray cinder-block house they rented around the corner from the garage. I didn't think they should've had to pay any money for it; I thought the owner should have paid *them* to live there. There wasn't much yard, and the clumps of green stuff growing in it were all weeds. It had a rusty chain-link fence around it, even in the front. The gate was only hooked on the top so it always hung crooked and wouldn't open or close. Most of the concrete walk that went up to the front door was crumbling, and so was the front porch. I thought concrete lasted forever, so I figured that house must be at least a couple hundred years old.

At first I thought they never cleaned anything, but I know they did. It just didn't show. And not to say anything bad about it, but the furniture that came with the house was dirty and faded, and every piece was different. I guess it was just a ratty old house all around.

But then I remembered that Miss Rose had gone there for her visit. She'd sat and talked to Jesse, and she hadn't said anything to Farrell about it afterward. That thought made me feel a little better as I walked home. Maybe she wouldn't think too badly of me, either. But I still wanted to do things right. You never knew what people would say around school.

By the time I got home, I had a plan. If my mama used to have a tablecloth on the table and flowers around like Ruby said, then that was probably the way things were meant to be. So first, I needed to find a tablecloth.

I didn't remember ever seeing one in the apartment, but I figured the best place to keep one would be in the chest that sat next to the table in the kitchen. It was big and old, and the drawers hadn't been opened in a long time, so I had to really tug on them. When I started rummaging through them, a musty smell came drifting out.

I found a whole bunch of little lacy doilies in one drawer. I made note not to tell Ruby about them because I sure didn't want those frilly things all over the apartment, and I knew that was just what she would do if she found them. In the other drawers I found sparkly glass salt and pepper shakers, some flowered cloth napkins, a couple of vases, a stack of square cloth things that I guessed were place mats, and a sugar and cream pitcher with purple flowers painted on the side. No tablecloths, though.

The bottom drawer was really stuck, and I had to sit down on the floor, put my feet on the front of the legs, and pull with all my might. It opened with a pop that knocked me over. I had found the tablecloths. I pulled them all out and stacked them on the floor. Near the bottom I found a white one that was so lacy it looked like it was made out of spiderwebs. That was the one Ruby had been talking about; I was sure of it.

I put the rest back and took the tablecloth into my bedroom for safekeeping. But I couldn't help trying it over my head in front of the mirror to see how I'd look as a bride.

Then I did something I'm not proud of, but I told myself it was OK because it was for our own good.

First I made sure Pa was sleeping on the couch like he usually was in the afternoon. I could hear him snoring. Then I tiptoed, as quiet as can be, over to the cash box behind the counter in the front office, opened it, and took out a couple of bucks. I folded the money and hid it in my jeans pocket.

The next afternoon I rushed home from school so I could catch Ruby before she left for the day. She was finishing up, and I'd never been so happy to see that big, jiggling fanny of hers as she carried the clean sheets into the storage room.

"Ruby?"

"Hmmm?" she grunted as she lifted the stack of laundry onto the shelf. I picked up the pillowcase she dropped and handed it to her.

"Miss Rose is coming for a home visit after school tomorrow, and you make such wonderful chocolate cookies . . ." Ruby gave the sheets a shove and turned around. I could see lots of dimples in her face because she was smiling. Her cheeks were red from putting the linens up high.

"I mean, they are really wonderful cookies," I repeated. She nodded. We both knew I was telling the truth and not giving her some flattery.

"And?" she said.

"And will you please make me some tomorrow so Pa and I can have a proper visit with Miss Rose? I'd be obliged."

"Why, sure, sweetie," she said. "I'll make extra. You know how Wendell is about my cookies. He's been pestering me for some the last few days."

I could have hugged Ruby right there in the storage room, but I didn't. She's not the hugging kind, and she's so big around, I wasn't quite sure how I'd go about it anyway.

"I'll put them on the table if I leave before you get home from school tomorrow. You know . . . coffee goes real nice with cookies. I'll make a pot just before I go, too. It'll be on the kitchen counter."

"Ruby, you're wonderful!" I said, and I meant it. She really did look out for me sometimes.

I spent the evening getting everything set up. I ironed the tablecloth and folded it careful and laid it across my dresser—I didn't want Pa getting it dirty before it was time to use it. I pulled a chair up to the kitchen cupboards and got down three dusty coffee cups from the top shelf. I washed them and the sugar bowl and cream pitcher from the chest and put them all into my room.

Then I took Pa's money and walked to the little store a few blocks away. They usually kept a bucket on the counter with roses in it, and when they used to ring up my order, I would take one out to smell the softness that came floating out of it. I was always careful to put it back in the water, so they didn't seem to mind.

"I would like to buy a rose," I said this time.

The clerk, some tall, skinny kid I'd never seen before said, "Sure. Pick one out."

So I put the bucket down on the shelf near the counter and looked them all over. They were like something out of a fairy story, and it was hard to choose. Finally, I picked a peach-colored one because it stirred a memory in me of the sun on the beach a long time ago when my mama was alive. I also picked up a handful of the little sugar packets from where they sold coffee because I remembered the empty flowered sugar bowl at home.

"How much for the sugar packs?" I asked.

"You can just have them," the tall kid said. "There's a huge box of them in the back."

I thanked him while he dropped them in a little bag. I paid for the rose and carefully carried it home. It dripped on my shorts, but I didn't care. I was pretending I was famous, and one of my many fans had given it to me.

Back at the apartment, I took the prettiest vase out of the drawer and filled it with water. That rose stood there in the vase looking so elegant and smelling so sweet. I set it on my night table next to my bed so I could breathe in its beauty while I slept.

That night I dreamed about my mama.

CHAPTER 17

The next morning I was sitting at the table eating breakfast when Pa came into the kitchen, all rumpled with sleep.

"Don't forget Miss Rose is coming for her visit this afternoon," I said.

"Miss Rose?" He said it almost like he didn't know who she was.

"Miss Rose. My teacher. She's coming for her home visit. I gave you the note day before yesterday. Don't you remember?"

"Of course I remember," he said, rubbing his chin. "That's today, huh?"

I could feel my face getting hot.

"You promised to get dressed up and be real nice to her. Ruby said she'd make cookies and coffee. Do you remember now?"

"Sure, I remember."

"Want me to pick out some clothes for you?" I put down my piece of toast and headed for his room without waiting for an answer.

I looked through his closet and took out a clean blue shirt. I couldn't find any nice dressy pants so I pulled a pair of jeans off the shelf and laid them across his bed.

"Those are what you need to put on this afternoon," I said, pointing. "She'll be here at four o'clock, and you need to look nice. This is important to me. OK?"

"Sure," he said with a little smile and ruffled my hair when I went past. I smoothed it out again with my hand and watched as he walked into the bathroom and closed the door. I wanted to believe him, I truly did, but while he was in the bathroom, I quietly took all of the beer out of the refrigerator and hid it under the couch. I was sitting at the table finishing up my toast when he came back out.

"I'll fix the house up when I get back from school," I told him as I picked up my books. He gave me a pat on my shoulders and a kiss on my forehead as I headed out the door. That was a good sign, I thought. I spit on my fingers and crossed them behind my back for luck. Maybe everything would be OK after all.

The minute school let out, I ran home so I'd have time to get things ready. I was surprised to see Angelique sitting on a tall stool behind the counter in the motel office, flipping through a beauty magazine and snapping her gum. She jumped down when I came in, pushed the sign-in book toward me, and took a pen from behind her ear.

"How do I look?" she asked. "Do I look like a real front-desk person?" Her hair was done up fancy on top of her head, and she wore a red blouse made out of some kind of material that sparkled when she moved. She had on her theater makeup, too.

"I guess you do," I answered. I'd never been in any motel except ours, so I wasn't sure what a real front-desk person was supposed to look like.

"I'm minding the motel while your teacher's here. Your pa asked me to." She blew a big pink bubble that popped over her nose.

"Thanks." I was happy at the thought that he'd remembered after all. "I'll save you some cookies."

Angelique did look pretty nice—very fancy for a place like the Cadillac Motel. Maybe Miss Rose would think so, too. I stopped short when I got around the counter, though. Instead of her spiky high heels, she had on the biggest, whitest pair of tennis shoes I'd ever seen. They had purple and blue laces tied in big bows, and when I went past, I saw she had drawn a happy face on the back of each heel and colored them bright yellow. I scooted into the apartment.

The cookies were on a plate covered with wax paper, and the coffee was hot on the counter, just like Ruby had promised. I took the lacy tablecloth I had ironed off the top of my dresser and spread it carefully over the table, walking around it a few times to check that it hung down the same on all the sides. It took me a couple more trips to get the rest of the things out of my bedroom. I put the coffee cups on the counter next to the coffeepot, filled the sugar bowl with the little sugar packs, and got the cream pitcher ready to pour milk into. I folded three paper napkins in half, neat as can be, and put them on the table at the places where Miss Rose and me and Pa were going to sit. Then I set the vase with the beautiful peach-colored rose in the middle of the table.

I stepped back to admire my work. Everything surely was elegant, better than the pictures I'd seen of fancy restaurants in magazines—and I'd done it all myself. I felt proud.

When I checked the clock on the TV and saw it was close to time for Miss Rose to come, I realized I hadn't seen Pa yet.

"Do you know where my pa is?" I asked Angelique as I climbed on the stool next to her behind the counter.

She thought for a minute. "He was out here talking to me for a while—dressed real nice, too—and then he went back into the apartment. But that was a long time ago," she added.

I went back in and checked the couch, but he wasn't there. Then I noticed his bedroom door was closed. I went up to it and listened. I could hear snoring.

"Pa?" I called as I knocked on the door. "Pa? You in there?"

I heard his voice, but it was muffled, and I couldn't understand what he said. I felt something cold grab my heart and squeeze, remembering all the other times I'd trusted him and he'd let me down. I opened the door. There he was, dressed in the clothes I had put out for him, lying across his bed fast asleep. Empty beer cans were on the night table and scattered on the floor, and a half-empty whiskey bottle was tucked between the bed and the night table. I ran across the room.

"Pa, you get up this minute!" I yelled, shoving him as hard as I could.

He grumbled, turned over, and went back to sleep.

"Pa!" I shook him and kept shaking him. I shook him harder and harder until the bed bounced on the floor.

"Get up! You have to get up!" I even hit his back a couple of times with my fist, although I regretted doing that. "Pa!"

He opened his eyes, and I could tell he was in his never-never land from beer and whiskey. This wasn't the way it was supposed to be. I could feel tears stinging my eyes, but I pinched them back. I just couldn't cry, not right then.

"Miss Rose is almost here," I said. "You have to get up."

He sat up slow and swung his legs over the side of the bed. Then he just sat there, staring around, like he was trying to place where he was.

Angelique stuck her head around the office doorway from behind the counter. "I think Miss Rose is here," she called. "She's getting out of her car."

"Stand up, Pa," I said, pulling on his arms. His shirt was wrinkled, and it was buttoned wrong. I started to re-button it when I heard Angelique say, "Good afternoon, Miss Rose. Eddie is right inside. If you'll wait here, I'll get her."

Angelique walked through the apartment and right into Pa's bedroom, taking it all in.

"Eddie," she said, "go talk to Miss Rose. And close the bedroom door on your way out." Then she muttered something that sounded like, "Come on, Danny-boy, curtain's going up."

I didn't take the time to ask her what she'd said. Instead, I dropped the front of Pa's shirt and hurried toward the office. Right by the door I stopped and took a deep breath. Then I walked behind the counter and out into the office where Miss Rose was sitting. She was wearing a dress with sunny yellow flowers on it and yellow earrings to match. She had dressed up special to visit Pa.

"Hello, Eddie." She gave me a big smile, like she was happy to be there.

"Please come in," I invited with a sweep of my hand like I'd seen people do on TV, trying to act like everything was fine. Miss Rose got up from the orange plastic chair and kind of glided behind the counter and into the apartment. She looked around.

"You can sit here," I said, quick-like, pointing to the chair facing away from the bedroom. She smoothed her dress and sat down. I knew that from where she was sitting she could see the back of the office counter with its messy stacks of paper and junk, but I figured that was better than having her see Pa in the bedroom if the door opened.

"The table looks so nice, and what a beautiful flower," she said, pulling the vase toward her and lifting the rose up to her nose. "Did you choose it?"

I nodded.

"Then you did an excellent job. Picking out a perfect rose

isn't easy." She carefully moved it back into the middle of the table.

"My pa isn't here right now," I lied. "I expect him soon, though. He had to go out, but he said he didn't want to miss meeting you."

Miss Rose smiled. "I smell some wonderful coffee, and these cookies look delicious. Do you think we might have some while we wait? I haven't had anything to eat since lunch."

I was grateful for something to do and jumped up. Right then, Ruby squeezed behind the office counter and came through the door, breathing heavy like she did when she walked to work. I was surprised to see her—she never came back once she left for the day.

"Hi, Eddie," she said. "I forgot something and had to come get it."

Ruby set down her purse and walked over to the table.

"You must be Miss Rose." She held out her hand. "Pleased to meet you. I've worked for Mr. Brown since Eddie was a baby. Here, Eddie, I'll serve the coffee. You just sit right down and talk to your teacher." Ruby went over to the kitchen counter.

I pulled out the chair across from Miss Rose so I could keep an eye on the bedroom door and sat down. I wasn't quite sure what to say.

"How did you get the name Eddie?" Miss Rose asked. "Evangeline is such a beautiful name."

While I told her the story about my initials and my made-up name, Ruby poured coffee and filled the cream pitcher.

She put a cup of coffee in front of Miss Rose and a glass of milk in front of me. I wondered at that because I thought I would have a cup of coffee, too, since Miss Rose had come to visit me. I didn't say anything, though. Ruby brought her own cup over to the table and lowered herself into the chair where there wasn't any napkin.

Right about then Pa's bedroom door opened, and Pa walked out with Angelique right behind him. Angelique closed the door quick, like she was trying to pretend they'd just come in from outside or something. Pa was walking real slow across the room, and just as Miss Rose started to turn around, he stumbled. Angelique grabbed his arm, and I saw Pa straighten and take a deep breath. They made it to the table by the time Miss Rose had turned all the way around. Pa smiled.

"Nice to meet you, Miss Rose," Pa said, taking her hand and shaking it. He sat down at the end of the table in the only empty chair. His hair was combed, and he had on a fresh shirt. Ruby brought him a cup of coffee, but it was only half full, I guess so it wouldn't spill easy.

I could see Pa was concentrating on what was going on. I knew he was trying not to drift off. I hoped Miss Rose wouldn't take notice.

"I've got to get back to work out front," Angelique said, now that Pa was settled in. "I'm the front-desk person." As she went through the door to the counter behind me, I leaned sideways in my seat a little so Miss Rose wouldn't spot the smiley faces on the backs of her tennis shoes.

While I ate cookies and drank milk, Ruby and Miss Rose talked. Pa mostly sat there, only saying things when Ruby would let him, and she didn't let him say much.

Miss Rose finished her coffee and turned to me. "We're going to do something special with the school chorus this year. Would you like to try out for it, Eddie?"

"No, thanks," I said, taking a gulp of milk. "I'm not much for singing."

"She'd love to," Ruby said. I gave her a dirty look, but she ignored me and smiled at Miss Rose. "We were just talking about that the other day. Her mother used to sing beautifully."

"Did she?" Miss Rose sounded really interested. "Then maybe it is something you would enjoy, too, Eddie."

I felt like giving Ruby a kick under the table.

"I don't think so," I said, draining my glass and popping the last of my cookie in my mouth.

Pa didn't say anything.

Miss Rose stood up. Pa did, too. Ruby leaned on the table and pulled herself up from the chair. Pa swayed a little, but I couldn't tell if Miss Rose saw.

"I've got to be going," she said, shaking Pa's hand and then Ruby's. "I hope you'll come to the tryouts," she said to me. "We need some good voices in the chorus."

"I'll see she doesn't forget," Ruby answered. She was still smiling at Miss Rose, but I'd know that stubborn tone of hers anywhere. She'd make sure I went, all right. There was no getting around it.

A couple of minutes later, I watched Miss Rose's car pull out onto Celestial Avenue and away from the Cadillac Motel. Angelique picked up her beauty magazine from the counter and went back to her room. Ruby put her purse over her arm.

"See you tomorrow," she said as she pushed the glass door open.

I turned and went back into the apartment. It was very quiet inside. Pa was still sitting at the table right where we'd left him, not moving and not really paying attention to what was going on. The lacy tablecloth was covered with dirty coffee cups, crumpled napkins, and cookie crumbs. I started to take the pretty little sugar bowl and creamer over to the sink, but as I picked them up, the fire just went right out of me. I'd never been so weary.

I looked at Pa and felt the tears creeping back into my eyes. They stung when I blinked, and my throat was tight with the effort to keep them in. But they wouldn't be kept in that time. My eyes filled all the way up and overflowed. I wiped the tears away, but they just kept coming and there was nothing I could do about it. I walked into my room and closed the door.

CHAPTER 18

The next morning, I put away the little sugar bowl and creamer, washed the cups, and took the peach rose to my room. I couldn't stop thinking about how bad things had turned out after I'd worked so hard. It seemed like no matter what I did, Pa just went around messing everything up.

But as I folded the tablecloth and laid it in the bottom drawer of the chest, I stopped being sad and started to get angry. By the time everything was put away, I was angrier than I'd ever been at Pa. Angry at the way he'd behaved. At the way he'd let me down.

I heard his bedroom door open and turned my back. I was in such a fury, I didn't want to speak to him. I didn't even want to see him.

"Ruby sure made some good coffee yesterday," he said. Behind me, I could hear the cupboard door open and his cereal bowl clunk on the counter.

I didn't answer. My hands were tight fists. The paper in the cereal box crackled, and the cereal rattled into the bowl.

"Miss Rose seems like a nice person," he went on. "And pretty, too."

I couldn't believe he was standing there, acting like nothing had happened.

"Evangeline?"

I picked up my schoolbooks and walked out the door.

I don't know if he noticed me go, but I didn't care. He didn't deserve an answer.

I watched Miss Rose like a hawk the next few days to see if I could spot some change in her. I was afraid she might say something bad about me or the motel, but she didn't treat me any different. All she did was smile and say she enjoyed meeting Pa and Ruby and Angelique and didn't Ruby make delicious cookies. I felt like I was holding my breath.

I was still holding it on Friday, the day of the tryouts for the school chorus. Ruby or no Ruby, I'd decided I wasn't going. She wasn't the boss of me, and I was tired of her sticking her nose into what I was doing.

Miss Rose stopped in the middle of the math class and looked at the clock.

"The chorus tryouts are being held in the music room beginning in five minutes," she said. "How many of you would like to go?"

A few hands shot into the air, and there was a buzz in the room. Farrell kicked the back of my chair, but I ignored him.

"Is that all?" Miss Rose asked. I could feel her eyes hot on me, but I looked down at my paper like I was concentrating so hard I didn't even hear her.

Farrell kicked my chair again. I turned around to whack him, and he whispered, "I'll go if you will."

"No," I said and faced the front.

"If you'd like to try out for the chorus, you may line up by the door," Miss Rose said. "Those who don't want to go will please remain in your seats and do all of the math problems on pages thirty to thirty-five. I'm leaving Carol Anne in charge, and Mrs. Higgins will be looking in on you."

I opened my math book and checked out the problems on those pages. They were long and boring. Really boring. And I didn't think I could stand even one minute of Carol Anne being in charge. I snapped my book shut. Almost anything would be better than that. I stood up. Farrell stood up behind me and gave me a shove to get me moving. If we hadn't been in class, I'd have shoved him back, but I just walked over to the line by the door and got at the end. Farrell stood next to me, and I accidentally stepped on his toe—hard.

We marched past the principal's office, which was next to the music room. Somebody had lined up chairs along the wall in the hallway. Miss Rose told us to sit there quietly and go in one at a time when she called our names. Then she went through the music room door, taking Selma Adams with her, since she was first in line. Mr. Reynolds had been in charge of music in the school as long as I could remember, and I could hear him playing "When You Wish Upon a Star" on the piano while Selma sang. She was hard to hear, though, and I was glad the piano was so loud. Maybe nobody would hear me either.

The other kids went in, and after a while it was just Farrell and me left in the hall. Miss Rose stuck her head out the music room door. "Eddie?"

When I stood up, Farrell gave me a little punch.

"Good luck," he said. I thought that was nice of him.

I hadn't been in the music room much since I was a kid. The first- and second-graders got to go there and pretend they were in a band by shaking tambourines and hitting metal triangles. I remembered I used to like playing band, but Mr. Reynolds would get mad at me because I liked to whack the sandpaper blocks together instead of rubbing them. Rubbing them didn't make much noise at all, but whacking them sure did.

That afternoon the music room had a circle of wooden chairs in the middle with little wire stands in front of each one. That's where kids learned to play instruments. Sometimes I would hear terrible screeching sounds coming out of that room and wondered how Mr. Reynolds could listen to that every day. I thought he must have a hearing aid that he could turn off when they played. It sure wasn't music—I knew that for a fact.

Miss Rose stood by the piano in the corner, and Mr. Reynolds sat on the little round stool in front of it. I wasn't sure just exactly what I was supposed to do.

"Come on over here, Eddie," Mr. Reynolds said. "I'm

going to play 'When You Wish Upon a Star.' Do you remember hearing it before?"

What a question! I'd heard it eight times while I was sitting in the hall, and it was getting on my nerves. I bet Jiminy Cricket never had to listen to it that much.

"Yes," I said.

"Here is a sheet of paper with the words. You can look at it if you don't know them."

I nodded.

He played some flowery music on the piano, then hit the first note hard as he dipped his head to tell me I was supposed to start. I started singing, hoping Farrell couldn't hear me. He was the only one from the class left in the hall, and I was grateful for that.

When the music stopped, I put the paper down on the piano. I could feel Miss Rose look at Mr. Reynolds, even though I couldn't see them do it. I wanted to tiptoe out of there so they wouldn't notice. I guess they were thinking I was about the worst kid they'd ever heard.

"Eddie? Would you sing it for us again?" Mr. Reynolds asked, giving me back the paper with the words on it.

Why didn't they just let me leave if I was so bad? I didn't want a second chance. I wished I had stayed in the classroom and done the math problems. At least there was a right and a wrong answer to those. But I was trapped. I took the paper, and Mr. Reynolds started playing. I sang again when his head dipped.

When the song was over, I saw them look at each other,

actually saw them do it, and got ready to run out of the room. Instead, they both broke into big grins.

"You have a beautiful voice," they said at the same time.

"Why haven't you ever tried out before?" Mr. Reynolds asked.

I shrugged. I wasn't about to tell him I didn't like school stuff at all and would rather be home with my books anytime than singing in some stupid chorus.

Miss Rose put her hand on my shoulder. "Just the other day I was told that her mother also sang beautifully," she told Mr. Reynolds, who nodded as if this was something important. "I'm glad you decided to come, Eddie. Now will you send Farrell in, please?"

I was happy as could be to get out of there. Farrell jumped up when I opened the door.

"You sounded great!" he said, and I felt good because it was coming from him.

"I'll wait for you," I promised as he ducked through the door.

I strained to hear him, but the piano was just too loud. How in the world had he heard me? Pretty soon the song ended, and Farrell came back into the hall.

"If you get chosen, will you sing in the chorus?" he asked as we walked back to the class.

"Will you?"

"I guess so," he said, "but only if you will."

He sounded like he really wanted to be in the chorus, though. Sometimes I could hear him singing quietly with the radio while he worked in the garage, and he really had a good ear for music.

"OK," I said. "I will, but only if they choose both of us."

Farrell smiled. "Deal."

That afternoon Mr. Reynolds taped up a note with the names of the kids who were chosen for the chorus. Farrell and I both got in. So did Selma Adams and Joey Johnson and three other kids from the class. Miss Rose told us we should all be proud. When it got down to it, I guess me and Farrell *were* both proud—we just didn't let anybody else know.

The chorus practiced singing together for the next two weeks. I watched Mr. Reynolds wave a little pointy stick around when we sang, and I figured sooner or later he was going to poke his eye out. Miss Rose helped Mr. Reynolds each time we practiced. Then I found out why.

"Miss Rose has an idea for something different this year," Mr. Reynolds said. "We're going to put on a program the evening before Thanksgiving."

That sure started a lot of whispering in the chorus. I guess they were all excited about the idea. And to tell the truth, so was I.

"We're going to tell you more about it next Friday," he said, "so we want to be sure everyone will be here that day. That's a week from today."

"You'll be here Friday, won't you?" Miss Rose asked me as I left the room. "It's really important that you are. I have a special announcement to make." She smiled a secret smile.

"Sure. I'll be here," I answered, because I truly did enjoy

myself when I went to chorus. That surprised me, but there was something about hearing the happiness in the music, tapping my toe to the beat and singing out as loud as I wanted, and nobody shushing me like they did when I was little. I could just feel the music tickling through my body and dancing around in my brain. It was such a joyful feeling.

I thought singing in the chorus was the first good thing to come along in my life. And since Miss Rose had picked me to be in it, I decided I might be willing to forgive her for some of the trouble she made for me . . . or at least not hold it against her quite so much.

I smiled at her. "Yep," I said. "I'll be here for sure on Friday."

CHAPTER 19

"I brought my basketball with me," Farrell said as we picked up our books at the end of school that day. "Miss Rose said I could keep it on her bookcase till school was over. Want to shoot some baskets?"

"Sure," I said, still feeling a special brightness from the singing that morning.

Miss Rose had already left the classroom. When Farrell reached for his ball on the bookcase, it slipped out of his hands and bounced across the floor toward me. I couldn't help it. I scooped it up and ran out the door and down the hall. Farrell was hot on my tail.

"Your shoelace is untied," he shouted.

"Ha!" I said. "No tricks."

"No, really," he yelled as I tripped over my shoelace and sprawled on the polished floor right outside the principal's office. The ball shot away from me and down the hall.

"You OK?" Farrell asked as he helped me up.

I nodded, and he took off after the ball. I sat down on one of the chairs in the hall. While I was tying my shoe, Farrell flopped down on the chair next to me with his basketball in his lap.

"Better do the other one, too," he said. I started to tell him to mind his own business, when I looked down and saw he was right.

As I leaned over and pulled at the laces, I could hear voices coming from Mr. Miller's office next to us. The door to the principal's office was partly open.

"OK, I'm done," I said, getting up. "Let's go."

"Sh-h-h-h!" Farrell was frozen to his seat like one of those statues they dress up in the department stores.

"What?"

He was listening to what was going on inside the office, and his face was white. I sat back down and listened, too.

". . . and I couldn't believe the poor living conditions of some of my students. . . ." It was Miss Rose talking. "It's distressing. It's outrageous. No wonder they're having trouble learning and adjusting to social situations."

I held my breath, I was listening so hard. Was she talking about me? Farrell hadn't moved. He was holding his breath, too.

"I have to do something," Miss Rose said. "I can't let this go on. My home visits finish up on Friday next week. Then I'll have to call Social Services. I think they need to step in. . . ."

Mr. Miller said something, but I couldn't hear what it was. Then their voices got softer, and I couldn't make anything out. They must have walked over to the window or turned their backs or something.

Miss Rose had been talking about me and Pa and the Cadillac Motel. I knew it. I looked at Farrell, and he looked at me. Neither of us said anything. Then he finally spoke. "I don't feel like basketball this afternoon, do you?"

"No." I picked up my books. "Let's go."

We walked the whole way back to the motel without saying a word. I'll bet we could've reached up and touched the gray clouds that were hanging over our heads. We each swiped a soda from the cooler in the office and went to sit on the chairs outside Room 12. Usually I would have sent him away so I could think things out, but this time something stopped me. It was like he was afraid, too—maybe more afraid than me.

"Did you hear what she said?" he whispered.

I nodded. Farrell studied his soda can.

"Miss Rose is going to call Social Services on me," he said. "They're going to send me away like they did before. I know it."

The way he said it sent chills all the way down to my toes.

"You mean to a foster place like they sent you after your mama died?"

He was quiet.

"Why'd they send you there, anyway?"

He waited a while, like he was trying to make up his mind

whether to tell me or not. Finally he turned and looked me in the eye. It gave me a start, that's for sure, but I didn't budge.

"After Ma died, Daddy was never home. He was always at work or out with his friends. I guess the house got to be a real mess—junk everywhere—and he left me all by myself. I was just a little kid." Farrell looked down at his hands. "The lady next door called Social Services, and some people came and saw the terrible state the house was in. I think that's why they sent me away to live with foster families."

I didn't know what to say, so I didn't say anything.

"Sometimes my daddy would come and get me, and we would be together for a while, but then he'd go back to his old ways of staying out all the time, and I'd get sent to another family." He picked up his basketball and started juggling it around in his lap. "And now Miss Rose is going to call them again, all because of her stupid home visit."

"What happened?"

The basketball was still. Farrell turned away from me and looked over toward the pawnshop. He got a stubborn look on his face. "Just what I told you. They talked, and she left."

"And?" This time I wasn't going to let him off so easy.

His shoulders slumped, and his voice sounded tight.

"And I know exactly what she saw when she came," he said. "It was like before. Don't you think I *know* what kind of a place I live in? Don't you think I see the stains on the furniture and the dirty carpet and the chairs that don't match?" It was all coming out in a rush. "And her sitting at the table so pretty and nice-smelling and my daddy sitting there with engine dirt on his hands and grease on his shirt? And him drinking beer in front of the teacher? They're going to send me away again, I just know it."

He was quiet for a minute. "I won't let them do it. I won't let them because I won't give them the chance. I'll run away first."

My eyes jerked up to his face. He wasn't kidding. I didn't know that stuff about his house bothered him; he'd never said anything about it before.

"You can't run away," I said, afraid he really might try. "You don't have any money. You don't have anyplace to go, either. Besides, Miss Rose wasn't talking about you . . . or me."

The last was an outright lie, because I was thinking about when she came to visit, with Pa drunk and Angelique with too much makeup and smiley faces on her shoes, and Ruby sweating, even though it wasn't that hot. And the pink Cadillac butt on the wall, and the dirt outside the office where flowers were supposed to be. Oh, Miss Rose was talking about us, all right. I knew it, sure as I ever knew anything.

"I have a grandma in Atlanta," Farrell was saying. "Daddy doesn't ever talk to her, but I could go stay with her. And I can get money out of the cash box at the garage. Enough for a bus ticket." He turned as if he was surprised to see me sitting on the white metal chair next to him. "Eddie, if I go, will you come with me?"

"Me?" I asked stupidly.

"Sure. Will you come? We could go to Atlanta together and stay with my grandma."

Now I'm not one to run away from things, but I thought on it as I watched the traffic on Celestial Avenue. I was getting so tired of Pa and his drinking, of him letting me down and of me having to take care of everything. It was getting worse and worse. And now Miss Rose had found out.

I was sure Pa didn't want me anymore. All him and Jesse wanted was their chairs and their beer. Angelique had her stage job to keep her busy. And Ruby had Wendell and yippy little Magnolia. Besides, Ruby only came to the motel and took care of us because Pa paid her to. When I thought about it, I realized there wasn't any reason at all for me to stay there. And probably nobody would miss me if I *did* leave.

I suddenly felt like Farrell was the only person in the world who understood my life and cared about what happened to me. If he left, I'd be all alone, and even though I was alone before he came, this time it would be different. I felt like I'd have a hole in my heart if he was gone.

A thought was tugging at the corner of my mind, too. If those Social Services people sent Farrell away before because of the way things were at his house, they could do it again, easy. And the Cadillac Motel wasn't much better than the house he was living in now. I'd probably get sent away, too. I had to get out of Paradise before that happened.

I looked over at Farrell. He was waiting for an answer.

"Yes," I said. "I'll come with you."

Farrell didn't smile, but he let out a big sigh. I guess he didn't want to go to Atlanta by himself, and I sure didn't want to stay in Paradise all by myself.

"We've got to plan it out, though," I said, shifting in the chair. "If we don't do it proper, we'll end up right back here but in a whole lot of trouble besides. We have to do it so they can't find us."

He brightened a little. "We have a week. That's what Miss Rose said. She said she'd call Social Services on Friday after her home visits. We have to leave Friday morning, early."

I remembered that I'd promised Miss Rose I'd be in school Friday. It was the day of the important chorus Thanksgiving meeting and her secret announcement. But Miss Rose was going to get me sent away.

"Meet me here after supper tonight," I told him. "I'll bring some paper and a pencil."

Farrell stood up and stretched.

"See you later," he said, his ball under his arm as he started down the row of rooms. A few feet away, though, he stopped and turned. "I'll never let them send me away again," he said, his face more serious than I'd ever seen it. "NEVER."

CHAPTER 20

A while later, I took my school backpack and the bologna sandwich I'd made for supper and sat on the white chair in front of Room 12 to wait for Farrell. While I ate, I leaned back in the chair and looked up at the clouds and electric wires. I had on my new glasses. It was funny how I thought those glasses were so wonderful when I first got them. I could see the leaves and the grass and the birds just as clear as could be. But I didn't like them nearly so much anymore, because the peeling paint on the motel and the bits of trash and cigarette butts in the parking lot were so very clear, too. I guess there's just some things a body doesn't need to see that sharp.

Just then Farrell came walking up and plunked down on the other chair.

"All right," he said, getting down to business. "We need

to think this out proper." He reached into his pocket and unfolded a scrap of paper. "I looked in my daddy's office file and copied down my grandma's address in Atlanta. Daddy and her had a big fight after Ma died. He hasn't talked to her since, so I don't think she'll tell Daddy once we're there. We don't need to let her know ahead of time, either. I figure it's best if we just show up; then she'll have to take us in. That OK with you?"

He handed me the paper with the address. I unzipped my backpack, pulled out my notebook, and tucked the paper in the back. I rested the notebook on my knees and tried to think if there was somewhere else we could go.

"I guess I don't know any other place," I said. "On my pa's side I never did have a grandpa, and his ma left him when he was fifteen and never came back. I used to have a grandma and grandpa on my mama's side, though." I smiled, remembering. "They lived in South Carolina and used to visit us a lot when Mama was alive. They'd bring me little toys and take me places . . . kid places where there were things to climb and animals to pet and stuff like that."

"What happened to them?"

"They were killed in a car wreck right after Mama died." It still made me sad to think about it because they were driving back home after coming to see me and Pa.

"That's too bad," Farrell said, and then was quiet. I guess we were both thinking about how unfair things are sometimes. He reached over and took the notebook off my lap. "OK, then," he said, opening it. "We'll go live with my grandma." He wrote *Atlanta* big on the first line of a blank page.

"We'll need money—lots of it by next Friday. You got any?" he asked.

"No. You?"

"Nope." He sighed.

"I have an idea of where we can get some so it won't be missed, though." I was feeling smug because I'd already figured that one out. "First of all, every day we can both take a little out of the cash boxes at the garage and the motel. Pa and Jesse don't keep any kind of track of the money, and they won't even notice."

Farrell nodded.

"Then there's this little wooden box Pa has under his bed that he keeps locked. I think it's full of money. If we can't get enough from the cash boxes, I'll just take the wooden box."

I tried to sound like it was no big deal, but my heart twisted when I said it. There I was, Eddie Brown, talking about stealing from my own pa, and what was worse, telling Farrell to steal from his pa, too. I wondered what kind of person I was that I could even think of doing that. But then I thought about the Social Service people sending Farrell away again, and probably me, too, because of living in the motel like I did.

Farrell closed the notebook. "We can do it—a little cash every day. They'll never miss it, and we can give it back in a few years." He studied me for a minute. "Do you think we look old enough? I mean, aren't there rules about kids traveling or something?"

That hadn't crossed my mind, but I decided it wouldn't hurt for me to look older, just so there wouldn't be any trouble.

"I'll ask Angelique to show me how to put on some of her makeup," I said, but I couldn't help making a face. "She bothers me about it every time I see her. I think fooling with it is her hobby."

"Then ask her if she'll let us use one of her suitcases, too. Tell her you need it for school. We'll look more like grown-ups going on a trip. They always have regular-looking suitcases. And we'll pretend I'm your big brother."

I opened my mouth to tell him that we were almost the same age, so how come he got to be the oldest, but he was taller, so I guessed it was only right and closed my mouth again.

I was feeling tingly inside. Fact was, the whole thing was starting to sound like an exciting adventure. In a few days, the two of us would be out of Paradise and on our way to a new life with Farrell's grandma in Atlanta.

The next day I knocked on the door to Angelique's room.

"Why, sure, honey, I'll show you how to put on makeup," she said when I asked for her help. "Come on in."

I followed her through the door of her angel-and-star room and sat down on the bed. She flipped on the bathroom light and pulled the desk chair across the room and up to the sink. Then she got out a travel case and popped it open. It was filled with lipsticks, powders, and eye stuff—she probably had all the makeup in Riley's Drugstore stuffed in that little case.

"Come sit here in the light where I can see what I'm doing," she called from the bathroom. She was plugging in the curling iron when I sat down. The chair was too low for me to see in the mirror over the sink, so I was just going to have to trust her. Then I remembered I'd need to put the makeup on again by myself before we left for Atlanta.

"Do you have a mirror I can hold so I can watch what you're doing?" I asked. "I can learn better if I can see."

"Sure," she said, reaching over my head and taking one off the wall. She handed it to me, and I looked at myself. My nose was big and fat, and my whole face was a funny shape. I guess she saw how surprised I was because she laughed as she turned it around to the other side. "One side magnifies," she said, wrapping a towel around my shoulders. "Sometimes I need that to get my makeup on just right."

She was humming as she pulled the different plastic boxes and tubes out of the case. I hated fooling her like that. The three little glass angels she had on the back of the toilet were looking right at me. I leaned over and turned them around. "They might break," I said, pushing them to the other end of the tank.

"Good idea." She turned my face toward her. "Now hold still." She started humming again as she went to work on me.

I held the mirror up as best I could and watched every move she made. It truly was a complicated thing she did every day to get ready to go out. *I* wasn't going to do all that stuff when I got older, that's for sure. But there I was, sitting calm as can be, letting her draw on my eyebrows with a pencil. I never would've guessed it last week. Then again, last week I wasn't thinking about running away.

Angelique put little dots of some skin-colored liquid all over my face and then smeared it around with her fingers. She rubbed a tiny brush in the blue eye powder.

"Close your eyes," she said, brushing it all over my eyelids and up into my eyebrows.

After she had me make my lips tight so she could put some lipstick on me, she picked up the curling iron and started twisting my hair in it. I wasn't much for curling my hair, and Ruby had stopped trying years ago. Instead, Ruby took the scissors and trimmed my bangs and the back every time she thought they were looking a little shaggy. She left my hair alone and I sat quiet and let her cut it—that was the deal with Ruby.

"Someday I'd like to get me a license and work in a beauty shop," Angelique said as she dropped a warm curl over my ear and separated off another piece of hair.

"Why?" I couldn't imagine anyone wanting to stand around all day touching other people's heads.

"I just like to do it. I'm good at it, too. Wait till you see how pretty you look when I'm finished." She let another curl fall behind my ear. "I was thinking about asking your pa to let me mind the front desk some so I can earn a little money while I go to beauty school. I already have a good bit set aside and would just need spending cash. These late nights are getting wearisome." She sighed.

I caught her reflection in the mirror. I'd never seen her so tired.

"Now, just a little brushing here and some hair spray there. . . . Stand up. What do you think?"

She turned me to face the mirror above the sink. I didn't know what to say, because it sure wasn't Eddie Brown looking back at me. The person in the reflection looked almost pretty, actually, with her wavy hair pulled up and back like a movie star. Her lips were a nice pink, her cheeks looked like she'd just come in from the cold, and all her freckles were gone. I touched my hair in back, and it felt stiff.

"You look just beautiful!" Angelique said, admiring her work as she walked around me. "And didn't I tell you you'd look older?"

I know she meant it as a compliment, and I smiled at the thought. Then the memory of why she was doing it slammed into me, and I shivered.

"You cold? Here, let me turn off the air conditioner for a few minutes."

When Angelique went out of the bathroom, I stood there studying my face. I did look older. Old enough to buy a bus ticket to Atlanta? My reflection nodded.

"Could I have a lipstick and a couple of the other things so I can practice?" I asked as Angelique came back into the bathroom.

"Sure, honey. I've got plenty. Here, let me fix a little make-up kit you can keep for your own." With that, she began pulling things from the case and dropping them into a little flowered zipper bag. "Now you can practice all you want. Too bad Ruby's gone home. I'd like to show you off."

"That's OK," I said, grateful that Ruby had left. There was no fooling her—she'd wonder for sure what I was up to. In a few days it wouldn't matter, but I didn't need Ruby's third degree right then.

I thanked Angelique for her trouble and promised to practice what she'd taught me. She fairly glowed.

Farrell was sitting on a pile of old tires by the garage, poking a stick in the dirt, when I walked up. I took off my glasses and felt the curls to make sure nothing had blown out of place on the way over. Nothing had. Those curls were hard as cement. I kind of sashayed in front of him like I'd seen models do on television.

"So? What do you think?" I posed, hands on my hips with one foot sticking out so it pointed at a candy wrapper on the ground.

Farrell's eyes went from the stick in the dirt up to my face and held there like he was studying something weird in science class. I changed my pose and stuck the other hip out.

Farrell lowered his head and stabbed the candy wrapper with the stick. "I like you better the way you looked before," he said.

Well, if that wasn't just like him! And after all the trouble I went through, sitting there having gunk put on my face and having my hair pulled and cooked and cemented to my head.

"Farrell," I said, my lips not even moving. "The point

is . . . do I look older? Think about Friday. Don't you remember anything?"

"Oh, yeah." He dropped the stick and stood in front of me. "To tell the truth, you look a little bit like a clown."

That did it. I put on my glasses, gave him a shove, and stomped back to the motel. At least he could have said I looked nice. *I* thought I did. Or that I looked older. Or my hair was elegant all swept up like that. Or almost anything, other than I looked like a clown. I was doing it for him, so we could get away, so we could go to Atlanta, so he wouldn't have to go to a foster house again. I slammed my bedroom door.

A few minutes later there was a knock, and the door opened partway.

"Actually, you *do* look nice," Farrell said, his hand on the knob as he stuck his head into the room. "I just like you better without all that stuff on your face. Maybe a little lipstick to make you look older for when we get the tickets. That's all you need."

Then he said something nobody ever did before. "You're real pretty without all that," he added, quietly pulling the door closed as he left. "Real pretty."

CHAPTER 21

Every day I took a little money out of the cash box, hoping Pa wouldn't miss it. He didn't. I think that made me feel worse than if he'd noticed it was short and come at me with the strap. He trusted me, and there I was, his own flesh and blood, stealing from him. I had to keep telling myself that if he'd been a proper pa, he'd have known what was going on and stopped me. He'd have had some feeling his kid was getting ready to leave. He wouldn't have been drinking beer all the time with Jesse.

But he didn't notice anything was going on, and neither did Angelique or Ruby. It was weird. All the lives around me went on just like they always did, while mine was already different and about to change forever.

"You been able to get any money?" Farrell asked when we met outside Room 12 on Thursday, the day before we were going to leave. It was starting to get dark.

"Sure. How about you?"

"It was harder than I thought," he said, "but I have some. We need to spread it out and count it. We have to get the rest of the stuff ready, too."

I pulled a ring of keys out of my pocket. They were extras, and Pa kept them on a hook under the counter. I used them when I needed to clean rooms after Ruby left for the day. A long time ago, I had marked the master key with red marker so I could find it easy.

The keys rattled so loud the noise seemed to echo off the walls. I set them on my lap to quiet them. Then I picked the room key with the red marker out from the rest, stood up, and leaned against the wall by the door. I looked around. The cars and trucks going up and down Celestial Avenue were turning on their headlights. I didn't see anybody I knew walking near the motel or in the parking lot. Real quick, I unlocked the door, grabbed Farrell by the sleeve, and ducked inside.

The heavy curtains keep out daylight when customers want to sleep late, but they also keep the light inside the room when it's dark outside. I sat on the edge of the bed and turned on the lamp.

Farrell reached into his pocket and pulled out a wad of bills. He tossed them onto the bed next to me. I leaned over and got mine out of the night table drawer where I'd hidden them in the Bible. I regretted putting them there.

Farrell sat down next to me and smoothed out his bundle. Then we put both stacks of money into one big stack and started counting. We looked at each other. On the bed between us was more money than either of us had ever had in our lives.

"Do you think it's enough?" I asked.

Farrell shrugged. "I don't know. But just to be safe, can you get that box of money your pa keeps under his bed? I'd hate for us to get to the bus station and not have enough."

"Sure." I fingered the keys on the ring and found the little one Pa always kept there. It was exactly the same as the one he kept on the key chain he carried in his pocket, and I was sure it fit the little box.

Farrell started talking about our trip and how much fun it would be. He said how nice he thought his grandma in Atlanta was, even though he hadn't seen her in almost seven years.

"Angelique let me borrow her suitcase," I interrupted, walking around the bed to where I'd hidden it. I picked it up by the handle with both hands and slung it on the spread. It still had the countries-of-the-world stickers on it and looked very official.

"Bring your clothes over later in a paper sack," I said. "I'll put mine in one, too. That way you get half the suitcase, and I get the other half, and our stuff doesn't get mixed up."

"And don't forget your backpack tomorrow," he reminded me. "We still have to look like we're going to school. I'll stick some food for the bus ride in mine. We'll share."

I thought that was nice of him. By the time he was ready to leave, I was beginning to feel a little tingle of excitement.

The next day I'd be on my own, leaving the motel behind. I'd be going places I'd never been and seeing sights I'd never seen. It was going to be a real adventure.

We flipped off the lamp and checked the parking lot through the curtains. Nobody was there, so we figured it was safe to leave. I went into the apartment to find something to eat, and Farrell went home to get his stuff for the trip. Pa was still over at Jesse's.

I found a hot dog in the refrigerator and ate it with a glass of milk. Then I tucked some paper sacks under my arm, hurried into my bedroom, and closed the door.

I opened drawers and pulled out clothes. Was it cold in Atlanta? I didn't know. But it was beginning to get chilly in Paradise at night, so I tossed a couple of sweatshirts on the bed, along with some jeans and T-shirts. I figured I'd better take all of my underwear and socks.

The sacks crackled so loud when I opened them that I was afraid Pa would come see what I was up to. I stood still and listened. Nobody else was moving in the apartment. I quick put my clothes in the sacks and looked around the room to see if I'd forgotten anything. I'd have to remember my hairbrush and toothbrush in the morning. I spotted the little music box with the ballerina on my night table and the picture of Pa and me and Mama tucked into the mirror of the dresser. I couldn't leave them behind; I knew that for sure. I put the picture into the music box careful-like because I didn't want it to get bent. Then I rolled up the music box in my green sweatshirt so it wouldn't break. I would've liked to have taken the little lamp with the bear holding the balloons, too, but there wasn't room for him. I touched his head and ran my finger down his furry back. I would miss him.

Just then there was a knock on the door. I hid the bags in the closet, grabbed a book, and jumped on the bed.

"Come in," I called, studying the book like I was in the middle of something important.

The door opened, and Farrell's head popped in. "I left my stuff in the dirt next to the building," he said in a whisper. "Your pa's still over visiting my daddy. If we're quick, we can get it inside before he gets back."

I snapped the book shut and grabbed my own two sacks from the closet.

"Wait a minute!" Farrell said, pointing at the two stuffed bags. "What do you think you're doing? You can't take all that. We don't have room."

"But I need it all. . . ." Even as the words came out, I knew he was right. Angelique's suitcase wasn't all that big. "I know what," I offered. "We can take my pa's old duffel bag, too. If we're supposed to be going on a trip, we both need luggage. The duffel's in the living room closet. I'll get it."

Either it was a good idea or Farrell was tired of arguing with me over everything, because he agreed to it right off. I had to get on my hands and knees and rummage through the shoes and other junk on the floor of the closet, but I finally found it and dragged it out. Farrell took the duffel and picked up one of my sacks. I took the other one. Pa wasn't back yet, so we left the apartment through the office.

It had gotten dark and cooled off while I was packing. The lights of the cars flickered up and down the road, and the big arrow with so many burned-out bulbs flashed on and off, showing the way. Nobody stopped at the motel. For once, I was glad.

We made our way to the room with our sacks and got inside without anybody seeing us. We stuffed Angelique's suitcase with Farrell's sack of clothes and one of mine. My second sack, the one with the music box and the picture, fit into the duffel with room left over. We decided I would carry that one. The suitcase was heavy, so Farrell would have to carry it.

Our plans were made. We would leave the next day. We knew where the bus station was. We had our cash and our clothes, and Farrell would bring some food for the bus. All that was left was for me to get Pa's box of money from under his bed—a box of money he kept locked and that I had no business touching.

CHAPTER 22

We went out of the darkness of the room and into the bright glow from the porch light above Room 12. I locked the door behind us. I could tell Pa was still out because nobody was moving in the office and the WILL BE BACK SOON sign was on the counter.

"You've got to keep Pa visiting Jesse for a while," I whispered to Farrell. "I need to get the box out of his room."

"I'll try," Farrell whispered back. "See you tomorrow." And with that he hurried across the parking lot and down the street to the garage.

I took a deep breath. I told myself that I was just walking back to our apartment like I'd done a million other times. Past the white-painted metal chairs. Past the empty motel rooms. Past the different porch lights along the walkway.

Angelique's door was closed, but I slowed down to listen.

The radio was playing, and she was singing along. It was pretty awful—she wasn't even close to the tune. Funny, I'd always thought famous actresses were good singers, too. Hearing the music brought to mind the school chorus and whatever it was Miss Rose needed to see me about the next day, which was Friday. Well, I wouldn't be there to find out what was so important; I'd be on a bus with Farrell. I walked on past Angelique's room.

"Pa?" I called from the door of our apartment. "You here?"

Nobody answered. I checked on the couch and in his room and the bathroom, too, just to be sure. I was alone. I partly closed the door between the office and the apartment so it looked like the wind had blown it. That way, if Pa was coming, he couldn't see in until he actually got there. My hands were cold. I wondered how real crooks felt before they stole something. Not like I was feeling, I was sure about that. Maybe Pa had taught me something after all. I still didn't know what I wanted to be when I grew up, but I was positive that after that night, it wouldn't have anything to do with crime.

I didn't turn on the lamp in Pa's room, since there was enough light coming from the rest of the house. I got down on my hands and knees and reached under the bedspread near where I had last seen the box. A shoe was in the way, and then I felt something soft that made me jump. I lifted the edge of the bedspread for a better view and saw it was just one of Pa's socks. I did spy the wooden box, though. I grabbed it quick, stood up, rushed to my room, and pushed it under my pillow. It made the bed lumpy, but I didn't care. I just needed to catch my breath and rub my hands together to make them warm.

Right away I heard, "Evangeline? You here?" It was Pa. I sat down on my bed and leaned my arm on my pillow, trying to flatten it. Pa came to the doorway. "Farrell said he'll come by tomorrow to go to school with you. He said for you to wait in case he was late."

"OK, Pa."

"You all right? You running a fever? Come here and let me feel your forehead."

"I'm fine, Pa," I said, getting up and walking over to him.

He put his hand on my forehead and then brushed it with his lips. "Never could tell anything about a fever with my hand," he muttered. "Takes the lips to feel it." He started to leave. "Why don't you get ready for bed?" he said. "You can read for a while if you want. I can't feel a fever, but you look a little flushed."

"OK, Pa. Good night."

"'Night."

He closed the door, and I could hear him flip on the television. I sat on the bed and punched the pillow with both of my fists. What did he think he was doing? He couldn't make my life easy just this once, could he? Why couldn't he be drunk on the couch on my last night home? Or hanging out at Jesse's till late? Or lying across his bed with his head in that never-never land he liked so much? Why couldn't he do something to make me good and mad at him, to make me so happy to leave that I couldn't *wait* until morning? Instead, he had to be awake and almost sober and worried about me on top of it.

I decided there was nothing to do but put on the big T-shirt I wore to bed and brush my teeth. I turned on the little bear lamp and tried to read, but my mind wasn't really on it.

I heard Pa open a few beers and knew it wouldn't be long before he'd fall asleep. When I heard him snoring over the noise of the television, I got out of bed, tiptoed to the door, and quietly locked it. Pa probably wouldn't come back in, but I wanted to be sure.

My clothes were slung on the chair. I took the ring of keys out of my jeans pocket and the wooden box out from under my pillow. The box had to be full of dollar bills because it didn't jingle like it would have if there'd been change in it. I tried the tiny key in the tiny lock, and it turned as easy as can be. My heart was pounding. Would there be twenties? Or fifties? Maybe hundreds? I'd never touched a hundred-dollar bill in my entire life. Pa had kept that little box on his night table or under his bed ever since I could remember. That was a lot of years. It was probably overflowing with cash.

I wiped off the dust and lifted the lid. I had to move the box closer to the bear lamp to see better. It wasn't full of money; it was full of envelopes. I pulled them out, one at a time, and peeked in each one, checking for the green that would tell me I'd found the money me and Farrell needed for our trip. When I finally put the last one on the top of the pile, I sighed because there wasn't a single dollar bill in the whole box. Not a one. Nothing but envelopes with paper inside. We'd just have to make do with the cash we had. That was too bad, but I was also kind of relieved—I wouldn't need to steal more of Pa's money after all.

I picked up the pile of envelopes and put them neatly back in the box. As I was about to close the lid, I saw that they weren't just any old envelopes; they were letters, and they were addressed to my Grandma and Grandpa Hamilton. In the left corner of each one was my mama's name. The ones on top had a different return address, but the others had the motel's address in the corner. When I saw that, I thought my heart had stopped. They were letters from my mama to *her* mama and pa, the grandma and grandpa who were killed in the car accident right after she died. At that very minute, I was touching something my own mama had touched a long time ago. I didn't know what to do. Holding the letters felt like I was holding her hand.

I opened the first one. It was dated before I was born.

Dear Mama and Daddy,
*   Daniel and I had a wonderful time on our honeymoon.*
We lay in the sun all day and took long walks on the
beach after dark. Daniel's so romantic. He brought me
a rose every day we were there.

I put the letter down on my lap, trying hard to imagine Pa being romantic. I couldn't. Not my pa. Not with his scratchy beard and old-man T-shirts, his cans of beer, or his snoring on the couch.

But inside the letter was a picture of my mama and Pa holding hands on a beach, looking young and happy. I know it was them because they looked just like they did in the picture I kept tucked in my dresser mirror.

Another letter said:

> You'll never guess what we've done. Daniel and I are
> buying a motel in a little town near here called Paradise.
> The motel's not much to look at, but I know we can fix
> it up with some paint and flowers. It's called the Cadillac
> Motel, and we'll probably keep the name because it sounds
> so elegant, don't you think? It has a cute apartment in the
> back just the right size for us. We'll be living right where
> we work when the new baby is born. I know Paradise is
> where we belong.

My mama sounded so excited in that letter. It was like I could see the motel the way she saw it, see the way it might have been instead of the way it looked now.

In another letter she said:

> If the baby is a girl, we'll name her Evangeline
> Dawn. I got a baby-names book out of the library, and
> Evangeline means "good news," which she certainly is.
> We picked "Dawn" for the beginning of a new day and
> the beginning of our new life here in Paradise.

So that was why I was named Evangeline Dawn. Even though I'd never liked it and really wanted to be called Rita or Matilda (and for a while, Savannah, because it sounded so very glamorous), maybe it wasn't such a bad name after all. I pulled out another envelope.

I'm glad you could come for a visit to help out with the new baby last week. With her big blue eyes and dark hair, I just know she'll be beautiful when she gets older.

Me? Beautiful? I got up and walked over to the mirror. My eyes were still blue. I set the letter on the dresser, took off my glasses, and pulled my hair back off my face so it kind of piled on top of my head. I lifted my chin and looked down at my reflection, like I'd seen movie stars do in magazine pictures. But who was I kidding? I just wasn't the pretty type and surely not even close to beautiful. I let go of my hair, and it fell around my face in a tumble. When I put my glasses back on and could see better, I felt like I was watching the person in the mirror turn back into a frog.

I sighed and sat back down on the bed, picking up another letter. Inside the pages was a picture of Mama and me reading a book.

Evangeline talks all the time and sings. . . . My goodness, does she sing! We gave her a little music box with a tiny dancing ballerina in it for her birthday. It plays "Somewhere Over the Rainbow," and she's learning the words to it. The other day we were curled up in the big rocking chair with an afghan over us, reading her favorite book . . .

When I saw the picture, I remembered rocking with my mama's arms around me while we read. I was safe and warm. Nothing would hurt me as long as she was there. I tried, but I still couldn't remember the words to my music-box song.

My throat was beginning to ache, and tears filled the corners of my eyes. I wiped them away and pulled out the last letter.

I'm getting so tired I can't do much anymore. Mostly I sit here and watch Evangeline while she plays on the floor of my room. She'll be starting kindergarten in a few weeks and already knows how to read! I hope Evangeline will realize how much I love her and wish I could be there to see her grow up. Tell her when she gets older, will you? I want her to know. Please watch over Daniel and my beautiful Evangeline.

The letter was dated just a few weeks before my mama died. I carefully slid it back into the envelope and closed and locked the lid of the box. Then I put my face in my pillow as a big sob, one that had been held in there forever, came flooding up from my chest. I tried to get control. *I can't think about this now. I've got to get up on time tomorrow. I've got things I have to do.* But it didn't work. I couldn't stop those tears from coming and finally gave up trying.

My pillow was wet with aching for my mama that night when I finally fell asleep.

CHAPTER 23

The next morning, I was up before Pa. I made my bed and dressed in the jeans and T-shirt I'd laid out the day before. After I brushed my hair and put the brush in my backpack, I took the little wooden box out from its hiding place under my bed and slipped it into my backpack, too. I just couldn't leave it behind. I hoped Pa wouldn't mind when he saw it was gone, but I figured I needed those letters more than he did.

While I was eating breakfast, Ruby came in.

"Looks like you're hungry this morning," she said, eyeing my cereal and toast and big glass of milk.

"Not much supper last night," I explained, hoping it sounded true. I smiled inside. She'd never in a million years guess that I was filling up for a bus trip to Atlanta. The thought gave me some satisfaction, although I'm not sure why. I guess I just liked knowing something nobody else did.

"Don't forget the chorus meeting this afternoon," Ruby said, leaving for the supply room. "The note from Miss Rose said it was important for you to be there because it's about the Thanksgiving program."

"OK, I'll go," I called to her purple-flowered back as I drank the last of the milk and put the dishes in the sink.

In my room, I checked to be sure I had everything. After I brushed my teeth, I wrapped my toothbrush and toothpaste in a piece of toilet paper and stuffed them into the backpack next to the wooden box. The last thing I did before I saw Farrell at the office door was shove the ring of keys into my jeans pocket.

I debated leaving Pa a note but then figured he probably wouldn't miss me until evening, and by then I'd be in Atlanta. Maybe Farrell's grandma would let me call him from there.

Farrell stood in the doorway, shifting from one foot to another like he had to pee. His backpack was slung over his shoulder. When he turned, I saw it was puffed up fat and round. Honest to goodness, he had that stupid basketball in it. And he had the nerve to tell me I had too much stuff!

I came around the counter. "Stand still, will you? I need to say good-bye to Pa. Here, hold this." I shoved my backpack into his arms and went back into the apartment where Pa was fixing himself a bowl of cereal.

"Gotta get going," I said, leaning on the back of the chair next to him. "Don't forget I'll be late this afternoon. Chorus," I reminded him.

"See you later."

"Sure," I said. Then I just couldn't help it. I went around the chair and gave him a little kiss on his prickery cheek. Boy, did he look surprised! I probably looked just as surprised as he did because I hadn't planned on doing that at all.

"Bye," I called, running out the door. I didn't hear if he answered.

Farrell pushed my backpack at me, and we started toward school.

"You can carry your own," he said. "What you got in there anyway? A brick?"

"Nope. Just something I needed to bring."

We walked down the sidewalk in silence. Most of the stores we passed were still closed because it was early. I've always liked being up first thing in the morning. The air smells good, and the sun makes flickering shadows on the walls.

After we'd walked a good ways toward school, Farrell's voice whispered in my ear, "Guess we've gone far enough. Let's double back. Did you remember the room key?"

I jingled the keys in my pocket as I tried to keep up.

"Hold on," I said, grabbing the back of his shirt and pulling on it to slow him down. Then I gave him a little shove into the hollow made by the entranceway of Lucille's Beauty Shop to hide us from view. The shop was closed and dark inside.

"Quit pushing," he said, shoving me back.

I was ready to slug him, but I didn't. Instead, I turned my

back, pulled out Angelique's lipstick, and turned the bottom of the shiny red stick. I put it on, using my reflection in the window. My lips felt greasy.

Farrell watched me and made a face. "Now what?" he said.

I popped the lipstick into my backpack. "You look that way, and I'll look this way." We stuck our heads partly out of the entrance. "See anybody we know?"

"Nope. You?"

"Nope."

"Then let's go. We'll get a couple of blocks away from here and then head for the motel the back way."

About ten minutes later, we unlocked the door to Room 12 and slipped inside. We hadn't seen Ruby or Pa. Farrell reached under the bed and pulled out Angelique's suitcase with the world travel stickers on it. I hoisted the duffel bag. We checked to see if the coast was clear, then tossed our backpacks over our shoulders, closed the door, and hurried around the end of the motel.

It was hard going, especially since we were trying to keep out of sight, and the bags were heavy. We passed more and more boarded-up buildings. Old newspapers and trash swirled around us and got caught in the doorways of stores along the way. Nobody was around, except for an old lady near the bus station pushing a shopping cart filled with sacks and junk. She was wearing a heavy coat even though it was hot and was talking loud to an invisible person. We hurried on past.

The bus station had green benches out front. Two men

and a woman sat on them, waiting. They looked bored, and I could feel them watching us when we walked past, like we were the most interesting things to come by in a long time. I didn't like that and sure hoped they'd forget all about us as soon as we were inside.

Getting through the door wasn't easy, though, because it was hard to pull, and our hands were full of our luggage. Finally one of the men got up from his bench.

"Going on a trip, are you?" he asked as he held the door open for us.

"Yes, we sure are," I answered, polite as I knew how. "Thank you."

He nodded and sat back down.

It was cooler inside, and darker than I'd have thought, what with the big glass windows. But they appeared to be tinted some and were pretty dirty, covered with fingerprints and dust, so maybe that was why.

When my eyes got used to the dimness, I saw that we were in a big, open room. It had orange plastic chairs lined up against the walls, with an extra row smack down the middle. The chairs looked so much like the ones in the motel office that I wondered if all of the ugly orange plastic chairs in the country had ended up in Paradise.

On the back wall of the bus station was a big square opening that seemed to go to some kind of office. Above it was a sign that said TICKETS. Me and Farrell set our luggage on the floor under the ticket window, and I pulled out our money. A short, bald man appeared behind the counter.

"May I help you?" he said.

I poked Farrell. Since he was bigger, we'd decided he would do the talking.

"I'd like two tickets to Atlanta," he said, sounding very grown-up as he took the money from me.

"One way or round-trip?" The little man put his glasses on the end of his nose and then tried to look at us over the top of them.

"One way."

I guess the man stood on tiptoe because he leaned over to look at me. "Can't sell tickets to kids. Your pa coming? I can sell 'em to him."

I felt a sharp stab of fear run from my head to my toes, and I think Farrell felt the same. You'd never know it, though. He hid it real well.

"Our pa is on his way," he said. "We were just going to get the tickets for him."

"Can't do that," the man said, sinking back behind the counter. "I'll wait for your pa." Then he stood on tiptoes again so his face was close to ours and whispered, "You kids running away?"

"No, sir, we're not," Farrell said, and we both shook our heads. Farrell pointed at the orange chairs. "We'll just wait for Pa over here. He should be along anytime now."

With that, Farrell picked up the suitcase and his backpack and sat down on a chair along the same wall as the ticket window. I took the duffel and my backpack and sat next to him. Right away I saw why he'd picked those seats. The man selling the tickets couldn't see us without leaning way over the counter.

I looked around the room. Nobody was paying any attention to us. There was a mother and a little girl by the big glass window. The little girl was leaning over the back of the orange chair and peeking out. Her hands were on the glass. I guess that was how it got so dirty—lots of people with lots of dirty hands. A man in a tight black T-shirt sat in the corner near us. His feet were sticking out in the aisle, and his head was tipped back against the wall like he was asleep. A teenage kid was sitting against the side wall near the window watching everything that went on outside. He looked like he'd just gotten a haircut because his hair was all slicked back, and his cheeks were pink like he was fresh from a shower. He was holding a rose carefully in his lap. The bottom of it looked like it was wrapped in wet paper towels with tinfoil over that to keep it fresh. I wondered who the rose was for.

"What are we going to do?" Farrell asked in a low voice. "He won't sell us the tickets."

I didn't answer right away because I was watching the man in the black T-shirt, the one at the end of our row with his head leaning back in the corner. He didn't appear to be really sleeping. In fact, I was sure he was watching us out of his partly closed eyes.

"Farrell, we need to think on it. Now be quiet for a minute."

I got out some paper and a pen and wrote, "Look at the

guy in the corner. He's not sleeping." I nudged Farrell and tapped the paper so he would read it.

He took it from me. Right away his eyes jumped to my face, then darted down the row of chairs. He followed that with a sweep around the whole waiting room to disguise that he was checking the man out. "Put the money away," he whispered, just as the guy shifted in his seat and sat up. I unzipped the pocket on the front of my backpack, stuck the money in it, and zipped it closed.

When I straightened up, the man was looking at us. He was all dressed in black, even to black jeans and black leather boots. He had stringy black hair that came down almost to his shoulders and a dark beard that covered just his chin— the kind bad guys wear in movies. But what sent shivers up my arms and down my back more than anything else were his eyes. They were the palest blue I'd ever seen. Completely faded out, like something that was nearly dead. They put me in mind of a dog I once saw with one blue eye and one brown eye. It wasn't natural, and neither were that guy's eyes.

We must have been staring, because the man nodded to us, pulled his feet out of the aisle, and slid down the row of chairs until he was sitting next to Farrell.

"It appears you two have a problem," he said in a low voice.

Farrell moved away from him a little, and I moved closer to Farrell.

"We're just waiting for our pa," Farrell told him. "I don't know what's keeping him."

"Look," the man said. "You know, and I know, that there ain't no pa coming. You two are on the run, and you won't get nowhere without some help. Now, here's the deal." He checked the window to be sure the bald man wasn't listening and lowered his voice even more. "You hand me your money, and I'll be your pa. I'll get your tickets for you. Hell, I'll even go to Atlanta with you, just to be sure you get there safe. I'm going that way anyhow. You got enough for your tickets?"

Farrell shrugged. "I don't know. How much are they?"

"Hold on. I'll check."

When the man stood and went over to the ticket window, I gave Farrell the full benefit of my elbow in his side. "What's the matter with you?" I whispered. "He gives me the creeps. We don't need him. We'll figure something out."

"Well," Farrell said slowly, watching the man. "I've thought on it, and I can't come up with anything better. If you're so smart, you tell me what else we can do."

I had to allow as he had me there. I just didn't like that guy, or his clothes . . . or his spooky blue eyes. There was something bad about him. I felt it in my gut.

The man sat back down. "I just told the ticket guy I was your pa, and I'd be getting our tickets to Atlanta. Next bus leaves in twenty minutes. The one after that's not until tomorrow morning."

"Give him the money," Farrell told me.

I shook my head.

"Sometimes my sister can be stubborn," Farrell said, pushing my hands away from my backpack and unzipping the zipper. I grabbed the backpack, but he yanked it from my arms and handed the man our wad of money.

"Be right back," the man said.

"What if he doesn't come back?" I whispered. "What if he takes our money and leaves? What'll we do then?"

Farrell was about to answer when the man turned away from the window and sat back down next to us.

"Here's what's left," he said, handing Farrell some bills and dropping a few coins in his hand. "I got us tickets for the next bus." He fanned three tickets in front of us. "Good thing I'm going to Atlanta, too. I can make sure you two get where you're going." The tickets said Atlanta on them, all right.

I reached out to take ours, but the man pulled his hand back.

"I'll keep 'em for now," he said, standing and putting all three tickets in his back jeans pocket. "If I'm to be your pa, I need to watch out for you." He sat back down and checked the clock on the wall. "Bus comes in fifteen minutes."

He studied us with those faded blue eyes for a while, then nodded. "Yep, we'll make a right nice family." His mouth curved into a little smile, but it didn't go to his eyes.

Then the man leaned back against the wall and appeared to go to sleep. I knew he was still watching us, though. Me and Farrell sat back in our chairs, afraid to say anything. This wasn't at all what we'd planned. And worse, there wasn't anything we could do about it. He had our tickets, and we didn't have enough money to buy two more. Farrell leaned his chin on his big round backpack. He wouldn't look at me.

A bus came and stopped out front. Nobody got off. The little man came out from behind the counter and hollered, "Tallahassee. Bus to Tallahassee now loading." He pushed open the outside door and hollered again. The people sitting on the bench stood up, stretched, and got on. The bus drove away, and it was quiet again. The boy with the rose was still there watching out the window, and the little girl was sitting on her orange chair, leaning against her mother like she was ready to take a nap.

"Won't be long now," the man in black said, lifting his head away from the wall and standing. "Gotta make a pit stop before we go. You two wait here."

With that, he turned and went into the men's room across the way. The heels of his boots clicked on the dirty floor, and I could see our tickets peeking out of his back jeans pocket as the door closed behind him.

CHAPTER 24

As soon as the men's room door closed, I jumped up. "Let's get out of here," I said, grabbing the straps of the duffel and hitching my backpack so it rested over my left shoulder.

Farrell didn't move. He still had his chin resting on the round backpack in his lap, and he was staring at the floor.

"Come on. We've got to go. NOW!" I dropped the duffel, grabbed a fistful of his hair, and yanked.

Farrell jumped to his feet. "Ow! What's the matter with you?"

"I'm leaving." I gathered up my stuff again as fast as I could. "And if you know what's good for you, you'll come, too."

Farrell had his feet planted far apart like the stubborn mule he was. He looked toward the men's room door.

"But the tickets—"

"Forget the tickets. They're gone. I don't like that guy, and I'm not going anywhere with him. Neither are you. Let's get out of here before he comes out of the bathroom."

I about went crazy waiting for Farrell. Once he got going, it was like he was moving in slow motion. I figured any minute that guy would come back, and we'd never get away.

"Grab the suitcase," I ordered over my shoulder as I ran across the room, the box of letters in my backpack slamming against my shoulder and the duffel trying to trip me with every step.

I rushed out into the brightness of the morning. The sunshine hurt my eyes and blinded me for a minute.

I ran down the street and turned the corner. I could hear somebody close behind me, but I wasn't about to stop and see who it was—I just hoped it was Farrell. If it was the guy with our tickets, I figured I'd be feeling his hand on my shoulder any minute.

I ran until I couldn't run anymore. Around the last corner I saw Eden Park. At the far end was a tangle of wild bushes and behind them, a tall cinder-block wall. I headed for the bushes and, quick as can be, ducked behind them out of sight. I heaved my bags onto the ground and bent over, my hands on my knees, trying to get my breath and keep from throwing up.

The rushing footsteps on the other side of the bushes got louder. I dropped flat to the grass, but I couldn't slow my hard breathing. Then the footsteps stopped. I put my hand over my mouth, trying to be quiet.

"Eddie," Farrell whispered from the other side of the bushes. "Where'd you go?"

Still puffing, I kneeled and peeked through the bottom branches. There were his legs and ankles and part of Angelique's suitcase. I stood up and pulled at the branches right in front of his face. He jumped.

"Back here," I whispered. "Go around the side by the wall."

In a second Angelique's suitcase appeared around the bushes, followed by Farrell and his basketball backpack. He threw them on the ground and lay down on his back, panting like I thought he would die. I flopped down beside him. All I could hear was my heart banging in my ears, while me and Farrell both tried to suck in all the air in Paradise.

It took some time, but pretty soon our breath got slower, and my heart went back to beating almost normal. I got up on my hands and knees and peeked out through the bushes. Nobody was in the park.

"Did the guy see you leave?" I asked.

"I don't know. I didn't wait to find out. Didn't you hear me behind you?" Farrell turned on his side and leaned on his elbow. "You could have waited, you know."

"I wasn't sure it was you on my tail," I said, sitting on my heels. "Besides, you can run faster than me."

"Not carrying Angelique's suitcase with all your junk in it, I can't." He stuck his foot out and kicked the heavy suitcase.

I'd forgotten all about the suitcase.

He dropped onto his back. I did the same.

A bird was singing right over our heads, and the breeze in the leaves made a soft, rustling music. I lay still so I could listen. There hadn't been many times at the motel when I could hear a bird because of all the traffic on Celestial Avenue. In fact, come to think of it, I couldn't remember the last time I'd heard a bird sing anywhere near the motel. But this place was so quiet, I could even hear some bird friends in other trees answering ours.

"What'll we do now?" I asked.

"We'll just have to try again. I figure we've got just enough money for two more tickets."

I knew he was wrong because the guy in the bus station took some of our money for his ticket, too. When I opened my mouth to tell him, Farrell sat up, reached into the pocket of his jeans, and pulled out some cash.

"Where'd that come from?" I asked.

"I emptied the cash drawer in the garage this morning before I left. Just in case." Then his face turned angry, and he slammed the ground with his fist. "That guy took our money. He had no right. That was *our* money and those were *our* tickets. I should've punched him or something to get them back."

"Are you nuts?" I sat straight up. I couldn't believe he was thinking like that. "He was bigger than us. He's a kidnapper and murderer for sure, and we were lucky as hell to get away." I knew I shouldn't swear, but sometimes Farrell just shocked the words right out of me. "Think about it. He tricked us, didn't he? He wasn't even *going* to Atlanta till we said we were. And then he took our money and bought himself a ticket. I'll bet if we hadn't run out of there when we did, we'd be lying in a ditch somewhere right now, deader'n roadkill."

I knew I'd never forget that man. When I thought about him leaning in the corner, pretending to be asleep and watching everything through mostly closed eyes, it was like he turned into a big black spider waiting for me and Farrell to come close so he could grab us. And he almost did.

"Did you see the color of his eyes?" I asked, remembering their pale blueness.

"Yeah. They sure put the shivers in me." He stuffed the extra money back into his pocket. "Tomorrow we'll be more careful. We'll pick out somebody different to buy the tickets, maybe some lady. The bus station guy said the next bus leaves first thing in the morning. We can take that one to go to Atlanta to find my grandma."

"But we don't have any place to stay till morning. . . ."

"We'll stay right here." Farrell looked like he thought he was really clever.

"Here? But . . ." I looked around our green fort. Except for the ants and mosquitoes, it really wasn't such a bad place. Nobody could see us from the park because of the bushes, and the cinder-block wall was hiding us from behind. I decided he might be right. We had our clothes, and if it got chilly at night, I had a couple of sweatshirts we could put on. We had food, and there was a drinking fountain and bathrooms in the wooden park building not too far away. It might work.

Even so, I wished we were already in Atlanta, and Farrell's grandma was making us some sandwiches. My stomach growled.

"What'd you bring to eat?"

Farrell pulled his round backpack over and took out the basketball. Then he dumped the rest of the stuff on the grass. There were six or seven candy bars and four really flat bags of potato chips.

"Is *that* what you brought for our trip?" I asked. I couldn't believe that's all there was. "We needed stuff to eat all the way to Atlanta. Lots of stuff."

"Well, what'd you expect? That's all the garage sells at the counter—just chips and candy. If you wanted something different, you should've brought it." He got that stubborn look on his face again as he reached for a candy bar, like he was daring me to make something of it. "If you don't want your share, I'll eat it."

I quick picked up a candy bar and peeled back the wrapper. Farrell did the same. It tasted good as it melted in my mouth.

"We'd better save these for later," I said, finishing it off and putting the rest of the candy bars and chips into the backpack. "We still have tonight and the trip tomorrow." I set the backpack next to the duffel bag and lay down.

It was getting hot. The branches of the trees above us crisscrossed everywhere, making a cool green roof. With the bushes around us, it was like we were in our own secret hide-out. The sun sent little flickers of light on the grass where we lay and on our faces. The grass was soft and smelled so good. I closed my eyes and listened to all of the park sounds I never heard at the motel.

I might have fallen asleep because all of a sudden I felt a fly crawling on my nose. I twitched it off, but it came right back. I opened my eyes, ready to smash it to kingdom come, and there was Farrell leaning over me with a long piece of grass, tickling my nose.

I grabbed him around his neck and pulled him to the ground. Then, using all the stuff he had taught me about fighting, I twisted and turned until I was sitting on his stomach with his hands pinned over his head. He struggled for a minute or two before giving up and easing back into the grass. I loosened his hands, and quick as can be, he flipped me over. Before I knew it, I was flat on the ground, and he was sitting on me. He raised his hands over his head like he'd won some great fight, and grinned and nodded like there was an invisible crowd around us cheering. I made note to get him back for that someday.

CHAPTER 25

We spent the rest of the afternoon in our secret hideout, only going out for water and to use the bathroom. People walked through the park, some kids played a game of ball, and a police car drove by a couple of times. We were deep in the bushes though, and nobody ever knew we were there.

We finished up the candy bars early on, so by the time the sun started making long shadows, I was hungry again. Farrell must have had the same thoughts. He got on his knees and stuck out his hand. "Give me some of the money from your pa's wooden box, and I'll sneak over and get us something to eat at the gas station. You can stay and guard our stuff."

I put my hand on my backpack, feeling the hardness of the box under the material.

"There wasn't any money in the box," I said.

Farrell's eyebrows shot straight up, and he sat back on his heels.

"What do you mean there wasn't any money? You said it had money in it." He looked at the square edges of the bulge in my backpack. "Then why did we have to drag it with us?"

"Because I had to, that's all."

"Eddie . . ." Farrell threw his hands up in disgust. He started to say something else but closed his mouth in a straight line instead.

I let go of the backpack and shot up on my knees so my face was smack in front of his. He wasn't the only one who was mad.

"You're not so great yourself," I said, hands on my hips. "You tell me why you brought that silly basketball of yours." I pointed to where the ball was lying on the grass by his feet.

Farrell glared at me. "Because I *had* to," he said as he turned his back to me and looked out through the bushes.

The way I figured it, it was as much his fault as it was mine. *He* was the one who had given our money to the black spider guy at the bus station.

I stood up, picked up his basketball, and was ready to march over and pitch it in the trash can near the bathroom building when I came to my senses and ducked back down. How would that help? Me and Farrell, we needed to stick together. We were all we had. Nobody else wanted us.

Slowly, I sank down on to the ground, letting the ball drop beside me. It truly was just us—just me and Farrell. All we could do was wait until morning. Then we'd be on our way again to find somebody who cared about us. I brushed my hair out of my face with my hand, and my stomach growled again.

"Eddie," Farrell whispered. "Come here and look at this."

"What?"

"Look at that car over there—the one by the gas station. Doesn't it look like the one sticking out of the wall by the office of the motel, only blue?"

I pushed some of the branches out of the way. It looked exactly like the pink Cadillac butt, and when it drove away, the lights in back went on and off just like the ones at the motel.

Farrell turned and reached into his backpack for a bag of smashed potato chips. He tossed me a bag, too. The wrappers crackled as we opened them.

"What's with that car butt anyway?" he asked, munching on some chips.

I sighed. "It was Pa's idea. When I was little, we took the pickup to the junkyard. 'We're going to get something so people will notice the motel,' Pa said. 'Then we'll get customers.'"

"Too bad you couldn't get the half with the engine," Farrell said with a grunt.

He sounded just like somebody whose pa had a garage, but I'd thought the same thing back then.

"When we got back from the junkyard, Pa dragged it out of the pickup and dropped it on the ground. Then he went inside and popped a beer."

I told Farrell how that rusty thing sat in the grass in front of the motel for weeks. I finally got sick of looking at it and went to the rack just inside the back door of Murdock's Hardware where they put old paint that didn't turn out right, ready to throw out.

"I found an almost full can that was a pretty pink. It took me a while to drag it back home because I wasn't very big. It was heavy, and the wire cut into my hand, but I did it and felt real proud. I just carried it for a bit, then put it down and rested, then went a little farther and rested again. When I got home, I took a raggedy brush from the shed behind the motel and started painting. I tried to be careful around the chrome and made sure I covered all the rust.

"I was just a little kid and thought it came out the prettiest pink car butt you ever saw. Pa didn't say anything when he saw what I'd done, but he and some men stuck it to the side of the building and wired it so the taillights went on and off."

Farrell handed me the last bag of chips.

"I hate that car butt," I said, opening it and setting it on the ground between us.

As we ate, I heard some scratching noises coming from the tree behind me. A little squirrel peeked his head around the trunk above our heads.

I picked up a piece of potato chip and held it out to him. The squirrel ran over and picked it up with his tiny hands. We tossed him some more chips, and he sat there with us and shared our supper. Finally he ran back up the tree.

Farrell crumpled up the wrapper and pointed to the little

wooden box. "What was in it if it wasn't money?" he asked.

I reached over and put the box on the suitcase between us. It unlocked easy with the key from my pocket. When I lifted the lid, Farrell leaned over to peek inside.

"Letters? What's so special about letters?"

"My mama wrote them. See? She sent them to my grandma and grandpa who died in the car accident. I guess that's how my pa got them."

"Let's read some of them," Farrell said, reaching into the box. I started to tell him to leave them alone, that they were mine, but I didn't. I just watched him stack them on the suitcase and open the first one. I guess I was ready to share.

"That you when you were a baby?" he asked, picking up a picture of Mama pushing me in my stroller.

"I guess that's me, all right." I took the picture from him and held it closer to study it before I gave it back. "That's my mama with me."

"Hey, you were a funny-looking little kid!" he said, making a face. I reached out to grab the picture away again, but he held it high and said, "Your ma is real pretty, though." I let him be.

He opened the letter. "Let's see what she says. . . . She calls you Evangeline like your pa does. How come they don't call you Eddie?"

"I told you before, I made the name Eddie up—from my initials. At school they teased me about being called Evangeline so I kept getting into fights. I figured Eddie sounded more like somebody they wouldn't want to mess with."

"Well, *I* like the name Evangeline," Farrell said, and I felt my face get warm at the compliment.

I found the letter that told about why my mama and papa named me Evangeline Dawn. Farrell said it was nice that they thought about it so much before they called me that.

"We'll ask Mrs. Jenkins at the library to look your name up in a book sometime," I promised, before I remembered we wouldn't be going back to Paradise or Mrs. Jenkins once we got to Atlanta.

"Your ma sure thinks you're special," Farrell said, picking up the letter again.

"'My little Evangeline never lets things get her down,'" Farrell read out loud. "'The other day she sat there working at it until she finally figured out how to put on her socks. Now she puts them on and off two or three times a day.'"

I showed him the letter where she told about how handsome Pa was, and the one where she hoped we would take care of each other when she wasn't there because we were a family. I found the picture of me and Mama reading in the big chair and set it on the top of the pile because I liked it best.

By the time we finished, it was almost dark and cooling off. I carefully put the letters in the wooden box and locked it.

Then I opened the suitcase and took out two sweatshirts. My brown one looked big enough to fit Farrell. I handed it to him and took the green one for myself. When I pulled it out of the suitcase, the music box my mama had given to me before she died tumbled onto the grass. It fell open and began to play quietly. I listened for a minute and then closed it so it wouldn't give us away, but hearing the music made me think of when she used to sing to me about going over the rainbow to a wonderful place.

I put the music box back into the suitcase. Me and Farrell pulled the sweatshirts over our heads and tried fluffing our empty backpacks to use for pillows. That didn't work, so we stuffed them with clothes from the suitcase and lay down. I put my glasses on the wooden box next to me. I could still hear traffic on the road and sometimes people cutting through the park, but we were quiet. We just lay there while the rest of the world went on the way it always did.

I wondered if Pa missed me yet or if him and Jesse were sitting around drinking and hadn't even noticed we were gone. Ruby usually went home before I got back from school, so she wouldn't know we weren't there, and Angelique would be dressed up and gone to Harry's Cabaret by now.

Nope, we'd been away since early morning—though it seemed more like days—and nobody even knew we were gone. They just didn't care. Then why did I have this sick feeling in the bottom of my stomach?

The tune from the music box played over and over in my head. I put my hand on the little wooden box and thought about Mama, and about us leaving the next morning. I wondered what she would think if she knew I was hiding in a park at night getting ready to run away from Pa.

I listened to the wind fluttering the leaves in our bushy hideout and watched the car lights flicker through the branches as they went down the road.

Finally I turned on my side and faced Farrell.

"Farrell," I said in a whisper. "I can't go with you to Atlanta."

CHAPTER 26

Farrell sat bolt upright.

"What do you mean you can't go? What about our plan?"

I didn't answer.

"Listen," he said. "This is what we're going to do. Tomorrow morning we go to the bus station and ask some lady to buy our tickets for us. Then we'll get on the bus and go live with my grandma. That's the way we planned. That's the way it has to be." His words came tumbling out faster and faster, and his voice got that little panic sound in it like it had when we overheard Miss Rose talking.

I sat up in the darkness and pulled a dead leaf out of my hair. I could just make him out sitting across from me. He was the darkest shadow in the blurry shadows of the bushes.

"I'm not saying *you* shouldn't go," I said, putting on my

glasses and bringing Farrell and the bushes into focus. "I'm only saying I can't go with you."

"Why not?"

"Because of what my mama said. I'm not a quitter. I've never run away from anything before, but that's what I'm doing now—running away. Running away from Pa and the motel, running away from school, and running away from the way things are."

"So? What's wrong with that?"

"It's not right. What I need to do is stay. My mama said that Paradise is where I belong. Maybe she was right. I need to find out."

"And just how do you think you're going to do that?" Farrell sounded angry and hurt at the same time.

"I don't know," I answered honestly. "I have to think on it some. But *you* can still go to Atlanta. Take the money for my ticket with you. Then you'll have some spending money for a while."

In the shadows I could see Farrell touch the rolled-up bills in his pocket, like he was checking to be sure they were still there.

"I don't want you to go back," he whispered. "Come to Atlanta with me, Eddie. Please? I want us to be together."

I hated saying it, but I knew I had to. "I can't go with you, Farrell. I just can't."

Farrell was quiet for a long time. Finally he let out a long sigh and pushed his hair back out of his eyes.

"When will you be heading back to the motel?" he asked.

"I guess I might as well get going now, before I'm missed." I stood and brushed grass off my jeans. "You want to keep the sweatshirt? You can if you want, since it fits you. It might get cold tonight."

"I guess."

"And," I said, snapping the suitcase open and unzipping the duffel, "you can take the duffel to keep your stuff in. I'd let you keep the suitcase, but it's Angelique's, and I only borrowed it." I took his sack of clothes out of the suitcase and dumped my clothes into it. Then I snapped it closed, stood up, and picked up my backpack.

Farrell stood next to me.

"Can you carry that?" Farrell asked from the darkness, motioning toward the suitcase. "It's heavy."

"I guess I can manage. I'll just go a little ways at a time, then stop and rest. Like I did with the pink paint can I told you about, the time I painted the car butt. I can manage."

"I guess you can, then." Farrell's voice was quiet.

"Well," I said, trying to sound brave so he wouldn't know my throat was aching with regret for leaving him there in the park like that. "I'd best be going."

"Sure," he said. He put his hands on my shoulders and pulled me toward him. My arms went around him, and I didn't want to let go. I was saying good-bye to the one and only friend I had in this world. I hoped the tears I felt filling my eyes wouldn't overflow until I was away from there. I stood back.

"Have a nice trip to Atlanta," I said. "Do you think your

grandma will let you call me when you get to her house?"

"Sure," he said. "I'll call you no matter what. Be careful going back. Watch out for trouble. It's getting late."

"I will," I said, slinging my backpack over my shoulder and picking up the suitcase. "Bye, Farrell."

"Bye, Evangeline," he said, using the name my mama called me.

As I walked around the bushes away from him, I felt a tear roll down my cheek.

The suitcase banged against my leg all the way across the park, and the corner of the box of letters in my backpack cut into my shoulder. When I got to the street, I set them both down. My nose was running, and the lights from the cars and stores were wavy through my tears. I wiped my eyes with the sleeve of my sweatshirt a few times, but they just filled right up again. I felt stupid standing there crying, but this time I couldn't shake it off.

Then I heard footsteps and a voice behind me.

"Here. I'll carry the suitcase. You carry the duffel."

I turned around, and there was Farrell.

"I don't want to go to Atlanta without you," he said. "I guess I'll just have to stay here and not be a quitter with you. Is that OK?"

Was that OK? Was he kidding? I could have hugged him right there in the middle of the block. I could have danced a jig or let out a war whoop. Of course, I didn't do that, but I sure wanted to. I had this big grin on my face when I nodded and picked up the duffel.

"We'd better take the back streets," he said, hefting the suitcase and leading the way. "Maybe we can both get home before they know we've been gone."

After we'd walked a few blocks, I turned to Farrell. "What about your grandma?" I asked. "Won't you miss staying with her?"

"Not really," he said with a little shrug. "I haven't seen her since I was a kid, and the address I found for her is really old. Don't forget she hasn't talked to Daddy since Ma died. I'm not sure if she still lives in that house or even if she's still in Atlanta."

I stopped dead in my tracks and threw the duffel onto the sidewalk.

"Then why on earth were we going there?" I demanded, feeling anger rising inside of me. "Of all the stupid . . ."

"Because," he said, slowing for a minute to look at me and then calmly continuing down the street, "I didn't have any-place else to go, and neither did you."

We kept to the narrow roads away from Celestial Avenue. We passed little wooden houses sitting on cinder blocks and sur-rounded by falling-down fences. Their windows were covered with cracked shades that glowed yellow in the darkness from the lights inside. Sometimes we had to walk in the street when the sidewalk had too many weeds or when there wasn't any sidewalk at all. Once a big dog barked at us when we passed a house with no grass in the yard, but he was tied to a palm tree and couldn't get at us. It was slow going, but we managed.

When we got closer to the motel, we decided to go at it from behind. That way we could slip around the end of it, put our luggage in Room 12, and then go back to where we were supposed to be without anybody knowing we'd ever been away.

We didn't have any trouble until we peeked around the edge of the building. After walking in the dark for so long, the brightness in the front of the motel burned our eyes. There were two police cars facing our direction parked next to the office. The red and blue lights on top of them were flashing, reflecting off the windows of the motel and the stores across the street. Their headlights were going on and off, too, shining bright right at us. I felt like a mole I once saw that came out of his dark hole and into the blazing sun by mistake.

It took a minute for us to get accustomed to the brightness, but when we did, we could make out a crowd in front of the motel. There was Ruby holding little Magnolia; Ruby's husband, Wendell; Angelique; and some other people milling around. Jesse was talking to one of the policemen. I ducked back behind the wall.

"Do you see my pa?" I asked Farrell before he pulled his head back around the corner.

He shook his head. "Don't see him. What do you suppose is going on? You think there was an accident or something?"

"I don't know." I peeked around the side again. I didn't see Pa anywhere. Where *was* he? Even in his worst drinking, he wouldn't have slept through this. A little knot of fear started growing in my stomach. Maybe he'd had a heart attack. Maybe he was hit by a car.

I set the duffel in the dirt just as little Magnolia came running around the corner. She barked and barked, then grabbed hold of my jeans near the ankle and wouldn't let go.

"Magnolia! Magnolia! Come back here!" I could hear Ruby calling. I picked Magnolia up and came out from behind the wall. Farrell was right behind me. The crowd of people stopped talking and stared at us. The lights kept flashing, but nobody moved. Then the policeman came toward us. He was really tall in his black uniform, and I could see a gun fastened to his belt. If I wasn't so worried about Pa, I'd have turned and run.

"You Evangeline and Farrell?" he asked. He'd covered that parking lot in about three steps and stood blocking our way. I tried to look around him.

"Where's my pa?" I asked, holding tight to Magnolia and starting to push past him. "I have to find my pa."

He reached out and stopped me. Farrell hadn't moved. He was watching the policeman.

"You Evangeline Brown?" the policeman asked again.

"Yes! Is my pa OK?" I was shouting.

"He's in the office," the policeman said, still holding on to me. "You Farrell Garrett?"

"Yes," Farrell answered quietly.

"Then both of you come with me."

As we started across the parking lot, Ruby came hurrying up as fast as her sausage legs could carry her. She grabbed me and gave me a hug that about smothered me and poor little Magnolia. When she finally backed off so I could breathe, I saw that she had been crying. That scared the daylights out of me.

"What's happening? Where's Pa?" I asked. "Is he hurt or sick or something?"

"Where have you two been?" she said at the same time. "Miss Rose was so worried and called your pa early this morning when you didn't come to school. She said you promised to be there for chorus." She wiped her eyes with a wrinkled handkerchief. "Both of your pas were frantic. They've been out all day looking for you two, and Angelique was, too. They looked everywhere." Ruby took Magnolia out of my arms and gave me another hug. "Your pa is just fine. And he'll be so happy to see you. He's waiting in the office by the phone."

I tried to run to the office to see for myself, but Wendell stopped me and gave me a hug. Then so did Angelique. She didn't have on her fancy nighttime makeup or her pretty acting clothes, and her eyes were smudged like she'd been crying, too.

I finally got through everybody just as I saw Pa coming out of the door to the office. He was rubbing his eyes, and they were red, but he was as sober as early morning. I was so glad to see him walking around and not lying dead in the street that I ran up and almost jumped into his arms. He laughed. It was such a good sound.

"Farrell!" Jesse called as he ran across the parking lot, but

Ruby got to Farrell first. When I looked, Farrell'd almost disappeared in Ruby's hug. All I could see was the top of his head and his eyes—they appeared ready to pop right out of his head. When Jesse got to them, he grabbed Farrell away from Ruby and gave him probably the biggest hug he'd ever had. He just wouldn't let him go.

Neither of us had been hugged this much in our entire lives, but it felt so good we didn't mind a bit.

C H A P T E R 27

A few days later Miss Rose asked us to stay after school.
When the other kids had gone, she pulled three chairs close
together near her desk and sat in one. We put our backpacks
on the floor and sat down across from her.

"I've been worried about both of you," she said, reaching
out and patting our hands. "Did you know that this afternoon they caught the man who bought your tickets at the bus
station?" We shook our heads. "He had escaped from jail in
Palmer City and knew the police were after him when he saw
you. He thought he wouldn't attract their attention if he had
two children with him."

I shivered at the thought.

Miss Rose's face was serious. "And now that you're back,
I want to be sure you are both OK and your fathers are taking good care of you."

We tried to tell her they were, good as they ever did, but I guess because of her home visit and us running away and all, she didn't believe us.

"I still need to call Social Services," she said, putting her arms around us. "It's something I have to do. But don't worry. Everything will work out for the best. I'll make sure it does."

I was scared the day an official-looking lady carrying folders full of papers came to the motel and talked to me and Pa. She asked lots of questions and wrote things down, then looked around our little apartment and the motel office and wrote more stuff in her book. After that, she went over to the garage and talked to Farrell and Jesse. A couple of days later, Pa and Jesse took the pickup to a building across town to see some other people.

But Miss Rose didn't let Social Services send us away or let anything else bad happen to us like we thought she would. Instead, the Social Services people made Pa and Jesse go to something called AA. Miss Rose said AA stood for "Alcoholics Anonymous." Pa and Jesse went to meetings there to help them quit drinking, and it must have been working, because I didn't see a beer can or whiskey bottle in the motel after that.

Then one day Pa walked over to me while I was sitting reading outside Room 12. His shadow fell on my book as he sat down in the other white-painted chair where Farrell usually sat.

I stuck a piece of paper between the pages to mark my place and closed the book.

Pa was quiet for a minute, kind of staring out at the traffic on Celestial Avenue. Finally he cleared his throat. "Evangeline?" he said, still watching the cars pass by.

"Yes, Pa?"

He turned his head to me, and he had worry wrinkles on his forehead. "You know those AA meetings Jesse and I go to all the time?"

I nodded.

"Well, I've been learning a lot of things at them. And one of the things we learned is that we need to make amends for the things we have done to people. I think I've probably done a lot of hurtful things to you with my drinking." He looked down and studied his hands. "Have I?"

Now, I could have just let it pass like I usually did and smooth things over and tell him everything was fine, but this time I could see that my answer was really important to him—more important than anything had ever been before. And when he asked that, I felt something pop inside me. A million bad feelings came churning up, making me sad and angry and aching all at the same time. A movie rushed through my head reminding me of all the times he'd broken his promises and let me down. It was time. I needed to tell him the truth.

"Yes, Pa," I said, looking him square in the face, "you've done some hurtful things." The worry wrinkles got deeper, but I didn't stop, and I didn't take my eyes off his. "Things like never answering my questions about Mama and leaving me to manage things. Things like not caring when I brought home my high test scores to show you and being drunk when Miss Rose came for her home visit. . . ." Then suddenly my voice trailed off, and I felt my throat tighten. I turned away.

Pa's hands came gently on each side of my face, and he turned me around to look at him. "I'm sorry, Evangeline," he said. "I did the best I could. When your mama died, I was so lonely and sad that I guess I forgot about everything else in my life. I guess I forgot about you." He pulled me toward him, and I felt his arms around me.

I couldn't help the big sigh that came from deep inside me because I knew then that he missed my mama, too. I felt my arms go slowly around his neck, and I leaned against him. He felt strong and safe, like a real pa. Like the pa in my mama's letters.

CHAPTER 28

The night of the Thanksgiving program, me and Farrell stood backstage while the classes of little kids did their part of the show. I had on a new pink blouse and even wore a skirt because it was a special night, although the material kept brushing against my legs, making them itch. Pa said I should have something new for the program and gave Ruby money for my clothes without me even asking. Jesse bought Farrell a fresh white shirt and tie, too, and Farrell looked so different, I hardly recognized him.

Miss Rose came behind the curtain and told the chorus to get ready. She was all dressed up and had on her jingly bracelet and smelled better than the Country Lilac freshener me and Ruby used on the motel rooms. She gave me a nice smile, and I smiled back as I walked to the front of the line.

I knew now that she really was like Glinda, the Good

Witch of the North, because of the way she looked out for me. The important Friday news—the news we had missed while we were hiding in the park—was that she had picked me for something extra special in the Thanksgiving program.

The little kids laughed and giggled as they came off the stage and ran down the aisles to their mommies and daddies.

"Ready?" Miss Rose asked the chorus as the school orchestra started playing our marching-in song. I had to admit they sounded pretty good, but I think Brian Yorkey's violin was a little sour. In a minute, though, it wouldn't make any difference. Nobody would hear it because the chorus could surely sing louder than he could play.

I led the chorus onto the stage and up onto the platform. The back rows marched up the wooden steps, making quite a ruckus. Then they were quiet.

We sang a couple of songs about Thanksgiving and being thankful for what we have. Then Mr. Reynolds announced, "Our next song will be a solo by Miss Evangeline Brown. She has chosen 'Somewhere Over the Rainbow.'"

Mr. Reynolds had found the words in a book for me, but I didn't need to learn them all over again—they had finally come back in my head from when I was little.

Before I could step down from the platform, Farrell gave me a sharp poke in the back. My hand shot around behind me and whacked him good in the leg, but nobody saw because my itchy skirt hid it all. Maybe skirts were good for something after all.

I shivered from excitement as I walked to the front of the

stage and smiled at the audience like Miss Rose had told me to.

Mr. Reynolds played the introduction, and I took a deep breath and began to sing. At first I was scared in front of so many people, but after a while I wasn't—I could almost hear my mama singing along with me, just like when I was a little girl.

I was glad for my glasses because I could look through the lights while I sang and see everybody in the third row. There was Ruby, all dressed in her Sunday best, squished into a seat next to Wendell.

Angelique had on one of the pretty skirts and blouses she wore when she worked behind the counter at the motel every evening. She'd decided not to be an actress anymore and had taken the ratty old HELP WANTED sign out of the office window and thrown it in the trash. She was a real front-desk person like she wanted to be. And in the daytime, she went to Betty's Beauty School to learn how to fix people's hair. I even let her fix mine for the program, and she gave me a few soft waves instead of cement curls—I think she was learning a lot at that school.

Jesse was there, too, sitting next to Pa. They both had on nice shirts and ties. Jesse was looking proud as can be at Farrell up on the stage, and Pa was especially handsome—kind of like in the pictures I had of him and Mama.

The song I chose was the one from my music box. It was about a place where troubles disappear and dreams come true—a wishful, hopeful song. It's nice to think that there might be such a place, but I know there really isn't. I guess maybe sometimes you've just got to make your own rainbows and find your own way.

After the program, Farrell came over to the motel with a peach-colored rose. It was wrapped in crinkly green paper and had a cloud of little white flowers around it.

"I got this for you, Evangeline," he said, suddenly looking like he didn't quite know what to do with it. He pushed it toward me, and his face turned red when I took it.

"Thank you, Farrell," I whispered as he hurried out the door.

It was the first rose anybody ever gave me. I'm going to keep it in a vase on my dresser for a while and then maybe press it in a book so I can have it forever.

But if it doesn't last forever, it won't matter. I know I'll still have Farrell.

That's because a few days after the concert we went to the library and asked Mrs. Jenkins to help us look up his name in a big book. Farrell means "man of valor." We didn't know what *valor* was, but Mrs. Jenkins said it meant he is brave and respectful and mannerly, like a knight in shining armor. And Godwin, his middle name, means "good friend." I take that to mean that we'll always be friends.

And if he forgets about the manners and the knight-in-shining-armor stuff, well then, I guess I'll just have to slap him bald-headed to remind him of how he's supposed to be.

GAYLORD RG